The NCC *Days*

DR. RAVI VANSHPAL

INDIA • SINGAPORE • MALAYSIA

ISBN 979-8-89277-870-1

Dedicated to

My Father *Prajapati Manoj K. Vanshpal,*

and everyone who is *punctual*, *diligent*, and *honest* at their workplace as a soldier.

Contents

Preface

The book *'The NCC Days'* is a collection of emotions that share memories of an unforgettable time at NCC (National Cadet Corps) in my undergraduate course. It was just a small portion of college life where we dressed in army uniforms and did parades along with our friends at the college premises. But as an NCC cadet, I witnessed firsthand the dedication and bravery of our armed forces and the NCC's impact on shaping young individuals into responsible and disciplined citizens. I hope to share the NCC's experiences and interactions with brave soldiers in this book, highlighting the values and lessons I learned there.

'The NCC Days' includes fourteen fictional stories that capture the essence of NCC life, emphasizing the diverse journeys and transformative moments of its members. The plots and characters of this book revolve around NCC cadets, disciplined soldiers, and astute officers of the Great Indian Army. In the stories, NCC plays a similar role in the background as a fictional village like *Malgudi*, which received its title from R.K. Narayan's *Malgudi Days*. I tried to

be as honest and unbiased as possible while writing this book, allowing readers to form their own opinions and interpretations.

A soldier is a country's asset because his every action is for the country. The liberty and prosperity of any country are due to the sacrifices of soldiers and their families, and no amount of money can replace those sacrifices. Honestly, I have no right to write about these characters because they are assets to our country. By donating the entire profit of this book to organizations that support soldiers and their families, I hope to contribute in a small way to show my gratitude for their service. It is important for us as citizens to recognize and appreciate the immense value that soldiers bring to our nation, and this book is my humble attempt to do so. It is my sincere hope that this book entertains readers while also reminding them of the sacrifices made by our brave soldiers.

The present book not only shares the experiences of the author but also provides juicy information about the army's life in the background of the NCC. The fictional stories, sequentially, reveal the cadet's life and take many unexpected twists and turns, keeping readers engaged and intrigued. The fiction enriches the NCC experience and offers a unique perspective on the challenges faced by its characters.

In the journey of book writing, it was difficult for me to recall all the events in sequence, but I am grateful to my friends, ***Yogendra Singh Bhadouriya***, ***Mr. Pranay Tandon***, ***Dr. Sanjay Parihar***, ***Dr. Anish Ghuraiya***, ***Mr. Kailash Phuleriya***, **Dr. Prabhat Sharma**, ***Mr. Sourabh Agrawal*** and ***Er. Ajay Vanshpal***, for their significant contributions to the completion of this book. I hope that readers will not only enjoy reading about our experiences but also gain a deeper understanding of the values and principles instilled in us through NCC training.

I am grateful to Lieutenant ***Dr. Arpan Bhardwaj***, Associate NCC Officer of the 2 MP Artillery Battalion, Govt. Madhav Science College, Ujjain. Dr. Bhardwaj's guidance and support have been precious in the creation of this book, and I am thankful for his expertise in NCC training. I am honored to have had the opportunity to work with him and learn from his vast knowledge and experience. His dedication to instilling the values of discipline, teamwork, and leadership in the cadets is truly commendable, and I hope that this book serves as a tribute to his efforts.

I'm also grateful to ***Dr. S. K. Ghosh, Dr. Swati Dubey***, ***Mrs. Shefali Chaturvedi***, ***Dr. Ram Prajapati***, ***Dr. Shweta Mishra***, ***Dr. Roopa Shinde***, ***Dr. K. K. Choudhury***, ***Dr. Nishchhal Yadav***

Dr. Suprajnya Thakur for their insightful comments and encouragement.

I am indebted to my wife, ***Dr. Ratna Agrawal,*** and family members for their unwavering support throughout the writing process.

Dr. Ravi Vanshpal

18, Atharv Enclave,
Ujjain (M.P.)
2024

Story 1

Samosa and Rasgulla

The story of the first day

Cadet *Romeo* speaking sir.

My school days had finished, and I was excited to explore the new journey of my college life. I was impatiently waiting for the start of classes in college, where I had already been admitted. Of course, the college did not match my expectations, and in front of the old building and an almost empty campus, I was disappointed at first. My heart was broken to see the ruined facility inside the college premises. Suddenly, I noticed a board with the word *'Unity and Discipline'* written on it, pointing towards the 2 M.P. Artillery Battalion's office. Curiosity piqued my interest, and I approached the office and saw an enclosed room on top of the college building. I anticipated it to be a tower constructed atop the stairway. The rusty lock appeared as old as the college itself, and there was dust everywhere.

As it was the first few days after the summer break, the college campus was not particularly crowded. I tried to find the class schedule, but I didn't get a satisfactory response; perhaps I reached the college too early. 10:30 AM was unquestionably the appropriate time to open institutions, but for opening and closing government institutions, some different time zones were considered. Around 11:00 AM, some hustle and bustle started on the college premises, but the location of the class remained unknown. After nearly two hours of waiting, I was informed that classes wouldn't start until Monday because the admissions process was continuing. I was disappointed to hear the news, but I also wanted to join the NCC.

On Monday, I took a quick tour of the college building and found that the college was a massive structure divided into two sections: the main building and the tail section. The main building included offices and classrooms, while labs and departments were located behind it. A driveway with a solitary garden connected the main building to the back gate. Although the main gate was closed, a dirt path led to the main section. I didn't know why the main gate was closed, but it was rumoured that there had been a terrible clash between students of the science and polytechnic colleges. The administrations of both institutions had decided to close the main gate and only allow admission through the muddy back entrances. The NCC notice board behind the locked door with the words "Unity and Discipline" emphasized its importance.

I decided to go to the NCC office after a quick tour of the college. I climbed to the third floor; of course, it was exhausting, but my orientation toward the NCC kept it interesting. I was patiently waiting for the office to open, which didn't happen for another month, but the hope light was turned on because the college staff was ensuring that it would open. Finally, the door was seen to be open, and two or three senior cadets were standing there. My face lit up when I expressed my interest in joining NCC, and a senior responded sincerely.

Why not? Which class are you from?

I said, "First year."

The senior replied, "All right, bring your classmates with you. We'll enrol and give uniforms to all of them."

I shared the idea of taking NCC with my friends and some of them flat-out rejected it, while others welcomed it. The next morning, the doors to the office opened. I and my friends received a form, which carried nothing more than general information and a self-declaration that included "If any harm comes to my life, I will be responsible for it."

After this brief formality, the senior offered to choose a uniform. I was excited to choose my uniform, but it was challenging to find shirts and trousers in my size among the numerous options. The more difficult part was finding shoes in your size, and both are similar. Over the next few days, I kept going to the office because I thought that the shoes on both feet were not the same. I wore the shoes several times and asked my friends if they found any difference, but my friends were also confused like me. This drama continued into the month ahead. I involved a variety of personalities to remove this confusion, including my mother, father, younger brother, and some teachers, but their responses were always ambivalent.

In a similar vein, the training was about to commence. The training schedule was posted outside the office: Friday and Saturday from 1600 hrs to 1800 hrs at the college premises. I was very proud of my freshly laundered and ironed uniform, along with my razor-sharp beret caps. My friends and I marched in full uniform towards the college premises. The cap was so curved that a stylish soldier's head should be held high with pride.

The NCC badge and red hackle were shining on the cap. The shoes were shining, and our footsteps echoed through the empty corridors, adding to the sense of pride and excitement. Our bodies were stiff with discipline and determination as we marched in perfect synchronization. The sound of our boots hitting the ground reverberates, filling the air with a sense of unity. We were making our way in front of the group of deer, like a pride of lions. Our chests puffed out with confidence as we marched, knowing that we were representing something greater than ourselves. The glimmer of our polished badges caught the sunlight, reflecting the dedication and honour that we carried with us.

But all of this was going to end because two army officers were present on the college premises to teach us. Both the soldiers were in green army uniforms and their stern expressions and disciplined posture conveyed a sense of authority and experience. I suddenly realized that we were about to receive top-notch training from these seasoned professionals. They were both *Maratha* soldiers, and I noticed that they both addressed each other as 'Major', the impressive rank of an army officer, and a secret code, which was written on their chest instead of real names. We had made the snap decision to call each other *'Major'* with the secret code instead of actual names.

Army soldiers instructed us to form a single row on the parade ground and informed our SUO (Senior Under Officer) for warm-up. Suddenly, our SUO issued the order, *'Kadamtal 20 times'*. As newcomers, we started to do the same things that other cadets were doing but we quickly realized that *'Kadamtal'* is a specific exercise for warmup. My heart was racing at full speed when it all came to a halt. After the warmup, we did some marching practice to form three rows throughout the college grounds. Suddenly, we heard *'Thumb';* We didn't know what it meant, but everyone had to stop. It was the first day, so we understood the essential instructions like 'Turn back,' 'Walk fast,' 'Stop,' 'Attention,' and so on. Our official training to become a soldier had begun; the shirt was getting wet with sweat. I realized that why only a few students showed their interest in taking NCC in a crowded college.

When the training for the day ended, we were listening to the army soldier sitting beneath a tree on the ground. One of them addressed, "Now you are part of the great Indian army, and it is up to you to maintain the dignity of the uniform. In the army, there are some sort of rules for everything, such as how to sit, walk, and eat, so always keep this in mind. Today is the first day of training, so I am giving you some rest, but we will perform hard training the next day." As we listened to the fact that today was only normal training and actual training would start the next day, most of the cadets started thinking about leaving the NCC, and some of them were planning to return the uniform.

It was probably 1800 hours, and almost the whole college was empty. We unexpectedly listened to the noise of scooters coming towards us, and we also experienced the strong smell of samosa. One junior cadet received a packet of Samosas and Rasgullas and quickly started distribution. The packet of leftover Samosas and Rasgullas was to be hung on the board with the NCC motto, *'Unity and Discipline'*, written on it. I was thinking of replacing the NCC motto with these two things. On the other hand, *Samosa* and *Rasgulla* were gradually coming to an end, but the plan to leave the NCC had already been finished. I answered to myself, who would leave NCC if someone got delicious *Samosas* and *Rasgullas* after all this hard work? But we're not there just for these two things.

Abruptly, we got the instruction to stand up, and the senior cadets of our troop quickly hoisted the national flag (Tricolour), the third important reason to be present there. A group of two cadets were cleaning the campus and collecting all the waste in a disciplined manner. We were waiting for the campus to be clean, and the *Tricolour* was fluttering like a brave falcon in the panorama of the sky. The atmosphere was filled with a sense of pride and patriotism as the national flag fluttered. The sight of the *Tricolour* waving proudly in the wind served as a reminder of our duty toward our country. It was a moment that brought us all together, united in our commitment to serve and protect our nation.

Our troop stood alone on the almost deserted college grounds. In the moment of silence on the ground, I thought it was a critical time for my country because our battalion only stood in front of enemies to fight, and all the other soldiers had left. The tricolour was standing alone in the deserted war zone, and all the respect was on my shoulders, so I proudly raised my chest. Suddenly, our SUO ignited the troop to give the necessary orders loudly, *'Savdhaan, samne dekhega'*. The haunting sound echoed through the empty ground, serving as a constant reminder of the challenges that lay ahead. As I looked over my shoulder, however, I spotted two familiar faces and friends, *Major Yogi* and *Major Tandon*, as proudly stiff as me. We all stood in the N-threes formation, and our SUO's commanding voice reverberated across the campus, instilling a sense of discipline.

Suddenly, the commander ordered the 'National Anthem'.

Our hearts were filled with pride as the familiar notes of the national anthem filled the air.

Jana-gana-mana-adhinayaka, jaya he

Bharata-bhagya-vidhata.

Punjab-Sindh-Gujarat-Maratha

Dravida-Utkala-Banga

Vindhya-Himachala-Yamuna-Ganga

Uchchala-Jaladhi-taranga.

Tava shubha name jage,

Tava shubha asisa mage,

Gahe tava jaya gatha,

Jana-gana-mangala-dayaka jaya he

Bharata-bhagya-vidhata.

Jaya he, jaya he, jaya he,

Jaya jaya jaya, jaya he!

Story 2

The Uniform

The story of the Independence Day Parade

We were enjoying the strict training at NCC that was moulding us into disciplined cadets, but the next important step was to memorize all the instructions perfectly. We were all working hard to improve our parade skills to reach the high standard of excellence that the Independence Day celebration required. We knew that our performance would not only reflect dedication and discipline but also respect for the nation.

Major Romeo, *Major Yogi*, and *Major Tandon* all were riding their bicycle to college for today's parade. In the middle of the way, *Major Tandon* suddenly inquired, “What significant event is going to occur on Independence Day?”

Major Yogi: “We are going to present the ‘Guard of Honor’ in front of *Brigadier Saab*.”

“What exactly is this guard?” *Tandon* questioned.

“Guard refers to the welcome-guest parade,” *Major Romeo* answered and continued to share his expertise in that field. “On Independence Day NCC cadets are going to show their loyalty and respect in front of the guests. When a higher-ranking officer or guest visits the army, it is customary to hold a parade in honour of him. The army has a rule and according to that the number of cadets will grow based on the rank and position of the guests. If a high-ranking officer visits, there will be more cadets there to welcome him. This system has been in use since British rule. Since our NCC is part of the Great Indian Army, we also follow the same traditions. This has been the common practice in the army since ancient times, when a king made a deal with a fortress or another kingdom, the king of the other kingdom would set up a loyalty program to respect the new king.”

As soon as *Major Romeo* finished his words, they all arrived at the college campus, parked their bicycles, wore their tangled caps, and saluted SUO, saying, 'Jai Hind, sir.' When they arrived, the parade had already begun. They saw the dummy guns displayed on the parade ground, and SUO was planning to conduct the marching drill with guns. All the cadets were excited to touch the gun, but before they did, the army soldier briefed them about it. Army soldiers first highlighted the importance of safety and responsibility while handling firearms. They also reminded us that weapons are strictly for training and not for any other use. We expressed our concern by puffing our chests and holding our heads high, saying, 'Yes, sir'.

The cadets got back to their work as the speech ended and focused on their gun salute. Conceptually, it was simple: just put your hand on the gun and say, "Jai Hind, sir." However, in actual use, things get more complicated. The cadets quickly realized that executing a proper gun salute required precision, coordination, and discipline. They were learning the correct posture, grip, and timing to ensure a crisp and synchronized salute.

During the parade, *Major Tandon* asked *Major Yogi*, why do we touch the gun while we salute?

Major Yogi answered flatly, "I don't know."

Major Romeo intervened and said, "I think in this salute, when a soldier touches the weapon, symbolically it means that a gun or weapon in my hand is perfect, and he shows his attentiveness."

Major Tandon bowed his head and said, 'OK,' in hushed tones.

The training continued till the evening, and in the actual setting, the gun turned into another challenge during the parade, along with the primary challenge of the cadets' uniforms. Only a few cadets got the proper-sized uniform. The rest of the cadets were left struggling to find a suitable fit; some were thinking about altering their uniforms, while others were purchasing new ones. The only tailor in the city sewed police and army uniforms, so it took 10 days to alter and 30 days to sew a new one. The delay in getting properly sized uniforms caused a significant disruption in the cadets' preparation for the Independence Day parade. Cadets were stranded with their uniforms and parade instructions. In this conundrum, that day's parade ended, and the ANO announced that the parade would be held daily till Independence Day.

However, the army uniform is made up of more than just cloth; it also includes a leniyard, nameplate, belt, shoes, socks, tie, and beret with plumage, which is equivalent to the sixteen adornments that a newly married woman wears. The uniform represents discipline and dedication, creating a feeling of respect and admiration. The intricate setup of the uniform added to the confusion for cadets who already struggled with learning instructions. Additionally, ensuring that each cadet had all sixteen adornments properly assembled was proving to be a daunting task for both the cadets and their instructors.

The training was getting harder as Independence Day got closer. In the morning, cadets went to the tailor's shop to get their uniforms, and during the parade, they had a hard time remembering the instructions given to them. On the other hand, students were struggling to understand the instructions because army soldiers were not trained to teach. Sometimes teachers tried different approaches if a student struggled to understand, but Army personnel couldn't, their primary focus was on combat skills and military training, rather than instructional techniques. Additionally, the high-stress and demanding nature of military life may limit the time and resources available for customized teaching methods.

As a result, our troop had been divided into two sections: the first troop included trained cadets and the other comprised an untrained battalion. Most of the juniors and slacker cadets were in the untrained battalion, which was performing a big circus on the parade ground. They were improperly dressed, their hands were not in line with the other cadet's hands, and they were making insignificant errors while marching in the parade. Turning left and right was the most difficult part of the parade. Their entire battalion was facing left, but some of them were facing right, which added to the laughter and exhilaration. Unfortunately, one of our friends, *Major Tandon*, was in the untrained battalion.

After the parade, on the way home, *Major Tandon* asked *Major Yogi*, "Do you still think I will be selected for the Independence Day parade?"

Major Yogi responded clearly, "No."

In the middle of this conversation, *Major Romeo* said, "Don't worry, you will be selected."

Major Tandon asked hurriedly, "How?"

Major Romeo: "Because, in ancient times, when one king attacked another, the army used to include these untrained farmers and civilians for war at a critical time, so don't worry; you will also be selected."

Major Yogi: "But, Romeo, do you know? how these inexperienced soldiers wreaked havoc on the battlefield. At one point, they left their king and ran away from the battlefield. You overlooked *Veer Shahid Hemu*, the second battle of Panipat, and what happened to them?"

The journey concluded with a big chuckle and a smile, and a few days passed in this manner, but on the designated day, it rained heavily in the entire city from midnight until morning. Cadets were struggling to arrive at college on time and in good shape. On the way to college, most of the cadets were filthy and their uniforms were wet, but they were determined to present the guard in front of the *Brigadier Saab*. Water had flooded the entire campus, and counting was underway inside the college building. *Major Tandon* and all the other untrained cadets became part of the ultimate guard in front of *Brigadier Saab* at the last moment.

Inside the veranda, *Major Tandon* asked a cadet, "I don't think today's event will be possible, and guests will arrive on time in this heavy rainfall."

The cadet replied, "But my concern is about the breakfast and how it will get to the college today."

Suddenly, our ANO *Captain AB* came to cheer up the cadets. My gaze was drawn to the two stars on his shoulders.

He started communicating, "Really, this uniform is not free; it has some responsibility, and today you commence your duty. I am proud of you, cadets."

He turned around and said, "You all look too fabulous today, like officers."

"May God save you from the devil's eye," he said as he adjusted a cadet's cap. One by one, he corrected the uniform of each cadet and loved and blessed everyone. After this cheerleading, he asked, "Are you ready?"

All the cadets unanimously responded, "Yes, sir."

The roar of the cadets filled the air with their strong voices and determination. They prepared to take on whatever challenges lay ahead. Suddenly, our chief guest, *Brigadier Saab* unexpectedly arrived, and after witnessing the cadets' courageous responses in the pouring rain, he decided to hoist the flag. The cadets were armed and ready, just like brave soldiers. *Brigadier Saab*, the commanding officer of our '2 MP Arty Battalion', raised the flag on the college grounds in the pouring rain. Each NCC cadet stood on the college grounds, presenting the Guard of Honor to *Brigadier Saab*. The ground was overflowing with water and bravery. My head was proudly raised as I saluted the guest with the rifle, and my sight was directed to the gallery of the college, where teachers and students were looking at us.

The uniform not only attracts brave cadets, but it also attracts the attention of someone beautiful. Amid the rain-soaked ceremony, a familiar face caught my eye from the crowd. Her mesmerizing smile reflected admiration for my dedication and commitment. As I caught her gaze, a surge of pride and determination filled my heart, reminding me of the pride that comes with wearing this uniform. After the Independence Day parade, *Samosas* and *Rasgullas* had ended, but there was also the start of a new love story. The uniform not only made this love story unique, but its influence extended beyond the realm of love and shaped the lives and aspirations of those who wore it with pride.

Story 3

Santri: The Watchman

The story of the tricksy cadet of our battalion

Our final exams had been completed, and we were all enjoying the summer. We regularly met at the bank of the *Shipra* River in anticipation of results and future discussions. As we sat there, basking in the warm sun, our conversations were filled with optimism and nervousness about what the future waited for each of us. The battalion unexpectedly informed us that an NCC training camp is being organized in our city, and anyone interested in attending will report to the battalion office. We all agreed to go to the camp after the encouragement of ANO, sir. We started preparing ourselves mentally and physically for the strict training ahead and were excited about the opportunity to attend the NCC training camp. We were getting ready to learn new skills, meet new people, and develop a stronger, more disciplined personality. We also knew that the NCC training camp would give us valuable experiences and knowledge that would help us in our future endeavours. We were eager to challenge ourselves and push our limits, knowing that the rigorous training would test our physical and mental capabilities. Despite our excitement, we were worried about the army's challenging training over the next ten days.

All interested cadets gathered at the battalion office on the designated day and received a list of mandatory and optional items that would be essential for the camp. We were all collecting our belongings and packing our bags. To ensure safety throughout the ten days, everyone needed to have the necessary equipment and supplies. We hoped to be well-prepared for any situation that might arise during training camp. On the appointed day, we all gathered at the battalion office, and an army vehicle was waiting to transport us to the camp. We were about thirty cadets from 2 MP Artillery Battalions, and our college was given ten vacancies for the camp. The camp we were going to attend was a training camp aimed at enhancing our military skills and discipline. We were excited because this was an opportunity to learn from experienced army personnel and develop a deeper understanding of our roles as cadets in the NCC. We were also excited about special camps such as tracking camps, river rafting camps, Republic Day parade camps, etc.

We were ready to go camping outside the battalion office and just before our ANO *Captain AB* came and cheered up our platoon for the camp and announced the name of our new camp senior. Our troop received a new commander with the rank of Senior Under Officer. *Captain AB* placed the rank (two black bars on a red background) on the shoulder of our new SUO in front of all the cadets. The cadets erupted in applause, showing their respect and admiration for the newly appointed camp commander. The presence of *Captain AB* instilled a sense of pride and motivation within us, further fuelling our excitement for the upcoming camp. While standing in line for roll call, we normally didn't talk but whispered amongst ourselves.

Major Tandon whispered: "I like this rank too much; one day I will wear this rank on my shoulder."

Major Yogi: "But I prefer having stars on my shoulder."

During this talk, two more cadets were promoted to under-officer and four more to sergeant. We (*Romeo, Tandon,* and *Yogi*) also served for a year without incident and were promoted to *Corporal* (even though we still refer to each other as '*Majors*'). As we proudly received our new ranks, we couldn't help but feel a sense of accomplishment and excitement for the upcoming camp. We knew that our hard work and dedication had paid off, and we were eager to prove ourselves as corporals. Little did we know that this promotion was just the beginning of our journey toward achieving even higher ranks in the future. We put everything in the truck and headed to the campsite. As we boarded the vehicle, a sense of excitement and anticipation filled the air. The journey to the camp was filled with camaraderie and discussions about what lay ahead. This intensive training program's challenges intrigued us.

The campsite was a horrible place; it was a large wasteland with nothing but dust everywhere. The barren landscape seemed to reflect the intensity of the training program we were about to embark on. Our truck was parked near a green army camp, which was the only camp there. We all arranged ourselves in N-threes (three columns of soldiers) in front of that haunted place. The warm dust that was blowing there made a horrible sound. The wind carried not only dust but also some dead leaves, indicating what would happen there.

Our SUO entered the Green Army camp to complete the necessary procedures. Following the formalities, an army soldier came out to count the cadets and show us where to pitch our tents. The temperature was close to 40 degrees, and we had three campsites reserved where we would pitch our tents. We set up the tent with the assistance of seniors till lunchtime. It was a challenging task, but we eventually found relief from the oppressive heat. The tent setup was our first opportunity to practice teamwork. This teamwork training was critical for us to learn how to effectively coordinate and collaborate. It taught us the value of communication and cooperation in difficult situations.

Before we even got a chance to put our bags inside the tent, our seniors quickly placed theirs on each of the four tent corners. This strategic placement gave them better air circulation and made it easy for them to get to their personal belongings. It showed how much they know and how much experience they have with making the best use of space and resources in a camp.

We proceeded to the canteen area for lunch after the tent was set up, and as was customary, we had to bring our plates and bowls with us. I noticed the seniors had big bowls and plates that collected satisfying meals without having to return to the buffet line multiple times. Finally, I got four burned *chapatis*, *daal*, and rice. we shared our meal all together seated on the ground. By lunchtime, a hundred or so cadets had arrived from all over the district. As I turned to face the cadet line, I realized why the seniors had such large bowls.

We were unhappy with the meal and made a complaint to Officer N.S., who responded, "My dear, tomorrow you will like this food even more because the food of today is of such a high quality."

"What will be worse than this food?" *Major Tandon* replied.

Major Yogi: May we complain?

Officer NS: No, don't do this childish action. It's a part of training.

"Part of training?" *Major Yogi* asked curiously.

"Yes, my friend, that is the sole answer to every difficulty in the camp," said *Officer NS*.

The campsite buzzed with excitement as more groups arrived, setting up their tents and exchanging greetings. The atmosphere became livelier with each new arrival, creating a sense of friendship among all the participants. The day was over without any important activity. After dinner, we were all settled and resting inside the tent. Some of us were discussing our disappointment with the meal, speculating if there would be any improvements in the future. Others were reminiscing about the delicious home-cooked meals they were missing. Despite our dissatisfaction, we knew that tomorrow would bring new challenges and experiences at the camp.

A tiring day concluded with lots of good friends around the tents. As we gathered around the campfire, sharing stories and laughter, we couldn't help but feel a sense of camaraderie and unity. It was comforting to know that we were all in this together, creating memories that would last a lifetime. As the night grew darker, we eagerly anticipated what tomorrow would bring, hoping for not only better meals but also new friendships and unforgettable adventures.

The next day began early, at 0500 hrs, with the constant roar of our SUO. He was yelling to cadets to get up and ready for physical training as soon as possible. We groggily stumbled out of our beds, still half asleep, but the excitement of the day ahead quickly replaced our fatigue. The hope of pushing ourselves physically and mentally, knowing that we were all in this together, fuelled our determination to give it our all. Within an hour, our platoon was dressed in white uniforms and ready to drop to the ground. The other cadets and their seniors had arranged themselves similarly on the ground. We noticed our PT instructor was from the *Maratha* regiment. He was six feet tall and in good health, taking note of the cadet enlistment for roll call. When it was finally our turn, our SUO proclaimed with authority, '30 cadets present, sir,' and everyone's attention was riveted. During roll call, both the amount of sunlight and the number of cadets on the ground were growing. The atmosphere was filled with confidence as the roll call continued. The sound of shuffling feet and muffled whispers echoed through the air, creating a sense of unity among the cadets. As the sun reached its zenith, casting a warm glow over the training ground, we couldn't help but feel a surge of pride in being part of such a dedicated and diverse group.

We got an order all at once, and we all ran towards the road with small steps. This short marathon ended on a big field after five kilometers. The cadets pushed themselves to their limits, their determination evident in every stride as they raced towards the finish line. The *Maratha* soldier again arranged us in the correct order and gave us instructions, saying 'Take a deep breath and move your hands individually to the back' If you performed this exercise twenty times per day, your chest would be as strong as metal. We also performed some push-ups and then started jumping like monkeys on the road. The final part of the workout was a 100-meter sprint back to base camp. Breakfast was the culmination of physical training, and while we were eating, *Major Tandon* said to *Major Romeo*, "Did you hear? We have to be ready for the drill parade within an hour."

Romeo replied, "How it is possible? I am going to take a bath first, and then I will be ready."

Officer NS responded, "Don't go there because bathing is prohibited due to a lack of water tankers."

Major Yogi replied, "Oh."

Officer NS: Last time, I took a bath only once during the ten days of camp.

Major Yogi looked surprised and asked, "How did you manage without bathing for so long?"

Officer NS chuckled and replied, "It's all part of the training".

As a result of this conversation, we were all dressed in a *khaki* uniform with beret caps and ready for drill practice. Throughout the day, the temperature kept rising, and the exercise concluded with lunch. Due to the hard work, lunch appeared to be far superior to the day before. We were all hoping for some downtime in the afternoon, but our camp's medical doctor scheduled a two-hour first-aid training for the cadets between 1300 to 1500 hours. Following the indoor training, we all reconvened for the roll call in the evening at 1800 hrs. Due to this hectic schedule, cadets rarely have time for themselves; that's why bath soap appeared among the optional items.

On the same day, I noticed that the cadets were trying to figure out how many more days were left in camp. *Major Tandon* calculated and said, "The day has come to an end and there are nine days left."

Officer NS, who was familiar with the camp, stated, "No, there are only eight days left because there is no PT or parade on the last day."

Major Tandon responded, "Truly, on the final day, no PT will be performed."

Officer NS: Absolutely, plus you'll enjoy a feast and a campfire celebration the day before the final day.

"Can we skip PT and Parade?" asked *Major Tandon.*

Officer NS: Never think about it; our CO (Commanding Officer) is very strict, not only about PT and parade but also on night duty.

"Night duty?" *Major Tandon* unexpectedly responded.

"Indeed, our unit has been assigned to today's night duty," *Officer NS* said.

"What will occur during night duty?" *Major Tandon* inquired to *Officer NS*.

"Cadet patrol five to six locations, including the kitchen, ordnance, and temple throughout the night," *Officer NS* responded calmly.

"One cadet the whole night," *Major Tandon* said abruptly.

Officer NS: "No, two cadets in a two-hour shift."

"I was thinking I would relax at night, but no, we don't have any relaxation even at night," *Major Tandon* murmured.

"Welcome to the training camp; let's see what happens next with you," *Officer NS* commented. He also added, "Indeed, the training camp is a rigorous experience that tests our endurance and dedication."

Major Tandon nodded, recognizing the challenges that lay ahead. Suddenly, a cadet fainted during the conversation. *Officer NS* immediately rushed to the cadet's side, calling for medical assistance. We'd just been trained for this dangerous situation, so we loosened the cadet's belt and took off his shoes, but the shoes were still attached to his feet. Finally, we all sought the assistance of the camp's medical officer. After an hour, that cadet returned to the tent with a medical prescription for four to five days of leisure and our SUO assigned the *Santri's* (watchmen's) duty to that cadet for the next five days.

The evening was getting darker, and we were all heading towards the mess for dinner after this awful incident.

Major Tandon said, "Sir, I am sure he was gimmicking; he has no difficulty at all; he will come for dinner after some time; you will see."

Romeo said to *Tandon "Hey Major,* you can see his condition; he is a skinny and delicate youngster; forget him."

Major Yogi said, "His name is also feminine, and you are a brave fighter; please forget his prank."

Officer NS said quietly, "*Major Tandon*, you have had only one chance to get relaxation from PT and Parade by becoming *Santri*, and you blew it."

The day ended with a long line of cadets in the mess with unsatisfactory food, but *Major Tandon* was dissatisfied with both, night duty and *Santri's* phony illness. At midnight, when the shift was changing, someone struck *Santri's* leg. But no one knew who that person was because there was no light inside the tent at night. The next morning, *Santri* was fighting someone else for hitting his leg at night. On the other hand, *Major Tandon* was getting dressed silently in front of the mirror outside the tent area.

Story 4

The Frenemy

The story of a traitor

The camp's conditions were deteriorating day by day, and we were waiting for the water tanker in the afternoon under the big banyan tree to wash our utensils after lunch.

Major Tandon asked, "Does anyone know when the tanker will arrive and when we will wash our dishes?"

Officer NS said, "Pretty soon."

Major Tandon: "I was expecting that, as usual, you would show your camp expertise here."

Officer NS: "Absolutely. I am speaking from my experience, and there is a reason for all this."

Major Romeo asked gently, "Will you please explain the reason?"

Officer NS: You can see the cooking utensils are grubby outside the kitchen, and people are waiting for the water tanker.

Major Yogi: Ah, right, they are also waiting for the tanker; the tanker will first supply water to the kitchen, and then we may wash our utensils. What a wild guess!

"Nothing is a guess, my dear; it's all about skills and expertise," *Officer NS* remarked. He also mentioned, "But today, you wouldn't get enough water for a bath."

Officer NS was the most experienced cadet in our group. He was tiny in stature but quite attractive. When he wore the uniform, he resembled an officer. He attempted many times to join the army but was initially rejected, not just because of his height but also because he had an additional finger in his hand. He was our college senior and friend, but he was unfamiliar with his acquaintances. Suddenly he inquired, "Do you want to bathe in peace?"

Major Romeo replied, "Why not because the last time I had only one bucket of water to bathe and wash my clothes."

Major Yogi replied, "My friend, you should never get more than one bucket of water in this camp, because one tanker per day is not enough for a group of three hundred cadets."

Officer NS: If one bucket of water isn't enough, you can swim into the nearby pond.

Major Tandon: "But also ready for punishment, as you all saw on last night's roll call."

Major Yogi: That punishment was so severe that no one will ever think about that pond again.

Major Romeo: But the pond is lovely, and its water pulls me in every day.

Major Yogi: OK, but keep in mind that two cadets patrol that pond every day, and since it is so near the camp, anyone can spot any new activities easily.

Officer NS: Actually, the punishment for that boy was appropriate not just for bathing but also for stupidity. This is not the only pond in this region.

Major Romeo asked quickly: Really, there are more other ponds nearby, and we can go there?

Major Yogi: Is it possible to counterfeit the patrol party?

Major Tandon: "Whatever but be ready to face the punishment."

"Punishments are for fools," *Officer NS* replied confidently. "A full-proof plan will give you a swimming pool as a gift."

The discussion concluded with the struggle for water at the tanker site to wash plates and bowls. The camp's bustle and lack of water were perplexing, and every one of us was constantly thinking about the pool. The idea of going to the nearby ponds seemed like a fantastic solution to the water scarcity issue. However, *Major Yogi*'s suggestion of counterfeiting the patrol party raised concerns about the potential consequences. *Major Tandon*'s warning about being prepared for punishment highlighted the seriousness of such actions. *Officer NS*, on the other hand, seemed confident in his ability to execute a flawless plan that would result in a swimming pool as a reward. Despite this discussion, the struggle for water at the tanker site continued.

On the same day, in the evening, the trio saluted *Officer NS*, saying, *'Jai Hind, sir,'*.

When a soldier or group of soldiers salutes an officer, the officer returns the salute with full respect. This gesture signifies the soldier's loyalty and respect towards his commanding officer and his commitment to the country.

Officer NS reciprocated the salute, raised his hand to give the salute, and said, Jai Hind.

"Sir, we want to go to that pool," *Major Romeo* replied.

Officer NS smiled and said, "If you want to go alone, as an under officer of the camp, I will not permit you, but if you want to go with me, you will require all essential training."

The trio replied, "Yes, sir, we are ready for training."

Officer NS replied confidently, "Training will start today; we all meet at 1630 hrs after roll call beneath this tree itself, but there is one enemy in our team; please find him."

Officer NS also called for dismissal and went to work, leaving us alone. The big question was whether we would get enemies in our group, whereas we were all very close to each other and would never think about cheating one another.

Major Tandon: "Do you still believe that the plan and training will work, and we can enjoy the pool without any punishment?"

Major Romeo replied modestly, "Don't worry, first we'll finish training, then we'll think about the plan, and lastly about the punishment."

"But what about the enemy? If he will tell the patrol party about our plan, what will we do?" *Major Tandon* said solemnly.

"Don't worry about the enemy and believe in each other; I think it's the first step to go for a bunk at the pool party," *Major Yogi* replied calmly.

Major Romeo responded humbly. "I also trust *Officer NS* because he is an intelligent man. We are safe under his leadership."

The meeting concluded with a combination of dread and excitement. Each of us had a sense of responsibility and determination to execute the plan flawlessly, knowing that our success depended on our unity and trust. We were focusing on the mission; our heads had to be prepared for the upcoming pool party, ready to face any challenges that could come our way.

We met *Officer NS* in the evening like burglars, near the temple after roll call, when the sun had set well before the hour and all the daylight was about to fade. *Officer NS* greeted us with a stern expression, emphasizing the seriousness of our mission. We listened intently as he outlined the details and emphasized the importance of discretion. He remarked, "I am happy to see you together, so you are ready because we only have a few days."

Major Tandon answered back, "Why?"

"Because in 02 - 03 days, any fool will find that place and finish all possibilities to reach there," *Officer NS* retorted.

Major Tandon spoke back, "It means the pool is not at the hidden spot."

Officer NS responded, "The location is not so secret, but how to get there covertly and without punishment is difficult."

Officer NS remembered something and asked, "Have you found any traitors in your group?"

"No, sir, we never lie to each other and are excellent friends," they all responded proudly.

Officer NS said, "OK, fine, but remember this when you accept punishment."

Punishment was the most heinous thing in the camp. We were all afraid, but the excitement of swimming overcame our dread of being punished.

Officer NS understood the situation and added, "Don't overthink about the punishment. Can you explain what the 'Own Position' is?"

Major Romeo replied hurriedly, "Sir, we can determine our position on a map or the ground."

Officer NS inquired again, "How do you determine true north? The compass is a useful instrument for this."

"We can find North, South, East, and West with or without a compass, Sir" *Major Yogi* responded.

Officer NS asked *Major Tandon*, "How can we determine the precise north without the compass?"

"By the pole star, sir," *Major Tandon* directed his finger to the pole star.

Officer NS inquired again: During the daytime?

Major Tandon answered, "With the help of the sun and the watch."

Officer NS smiled with satisfaction and said "Very great; I believe you are well trained for the pool party; keep practicing reading maps. The specific strategy and timing will be shared with you tomorrow at lunch."

He dismissed the training and left us alone, as he had done the day before. We were more terrified in the evening because we were worried about the traitor. We spent the entire night thinking about the traitor and the severe penalty. The next morning was routine, but we were dreading and motivating each other for the excitement of the pool party. As we gathered at lunch, anticipation filled the air as we awaited the specific strategy and timing that would be revealed to us. He explained the importance of teamwork and emphasized the need for clear communication during the operation. He also shared some valuable tips and tricks that would help us navigate through any unexpected challenges. As he spoke, our nervousness gradually transformed into a sense of determination, knowing that we had a well-thought-out plan to rely on.

He shared the plan in detail with a confident voice, "Today's schedule of camp is saying that any saint will give a lecture from 1400 hrs to 1600 hrs in the ground and our movement will start at the same time. We will divide into two little groups me and you three. I will not be alone; there will be another cadet with me, and this is the group that will go to the pool separately. The second group of you, all three, will proceed more separately to the pool area, citing the need to use the lavatory and you will reach a big tree after a long march. Under this big tree, you will figure out your 'Own position' with reference to the big electric pole, and then you will walk exactly one kilometer to 30 degrees towards the north. Now here I do not need to mention how many steps in the one kilometre."

Major Romeo replied, "Sir we will calculate the steps by the formula."

Officer NS, "Wonderful, then you'll easily find the pool, and we'll already be there."

In the end, he warned us: "At any point, if you feel that anyone is monitoring you or following you, abort the mission and go to the tent. You will not reveal your friends' names if you are caught in the pool area. Remember one thing when you go to the lavatory, remain aware of your surroundings and act naturally."

We divided into two groups around 2.00 o'clock noon and waited for the right time to move as per the plan. We carefully scanned the entire area, ensuring that no one was monitoring us, before proceeding further. The strategy was working, and everything was going as planned. We quickly read 30 degrees from a specific spot and reached the pool. The pool was truly a great spot, and the water pulled us in. The chilly water provided us a refreshing escape from the heat, and we swam and enjoyed. As we swam around, we couldn't help but feel a sense of relief and achievement. The tension from our mission melted in the water. There was one more surprise waiting for us: our camp senior was already there. We bathed for about 2 hours inside the pool, satisfying our thirst to bathe. We returned at 1700 hours, following the predetermined course and team.

On the same night when we were enjoying dinner together, *Major Tandon* boldly proclaimed to *Officer NS*, "There is no traitor in our squad; we all returned safely without any punishment."

"The enemy was present in your group, but you did not recognize him," *Officer NS* responded.

Major Tandon was unable to understand the exact meaning of *Officer NS's* comment.

The next morning, he reached *Officer NS* and saluted him properly: "Sir, I have identified the traitor."

Officer NS: Tell me what you identify.

Major Tandon: "Fear is our enemy, and it can turn us into a traitor."

"Yes, same as overconfidence," *Officer NS* replied. "Remember when you think of going to the pond next time."

Officer NS proceeded in the same manner as his style, but his response perplexed *Major Tandon*. He wondered how fear and overconfidence were related to each other in identifying the traitor.

Story 5

The King and The Pawn

The tale of how Colonel Saab revealed the answer to a question that had been plaguing our young minds

A young soldier's death was tragic news for our city. The entire city mourned the loss of the young soldier, and the atmosphere was heavy with grief. People were lining the streets to pay their respects, their faces showing sorrow and gratitude for this young soldier's sacrifice. When a martyr was declared, it was standard procedure for all military and police units to pay tribute to them. Our battalion was also prepared to present the honors in a dignified manner. *Colonel Saab* of our unit had ordered all colleges and cadets to report to the unit on the funeral day. We were all at college together when we heard that tragic news and headed home to prepare our uniforms for the next day's gathering. Suddenly, a student named Charlie asked *Major Romeo*, "Are you all going to Kerela for tracking camp next week?".

Yes, *Major Romeo* replied.

Cadet Charlie: Will *Santri* go with you, too?

Major Romeo replied, "Yes, but the next day we will give our last salute to a brave soldier who fought for our country until the end, so please leave us; we are in a hurry."

Cadet Charlie said mournfully, "Yes, it's sad news."

Major Romeo said, "No, it's a pride moment for our city and country too."

"But his death will be extremely painful for his family," *Cadet Charlie* said.

Major Romeo empathetically responded, "I understand that it will be a difficult time for his family, but the fallen hero's sacrifice will always be remembered and honoured."

Major Yogi responded, "If everyone is concerned for family, then who will fight for the country?"

Cadet Charlie asked *Major Yogi*, "Do you want to leave your family in this trouble?"

Major Yogi paused for a moment, contemplating *Cadet Charlie*'s question; then he replied, "Leaving my family would indeed be difficult, but sometimes sacrifices need to be made for the noble cause and the safety of our nation." *Major Romeo* nodded in agreement, adding, "It's a tough decision, but it's important to remember that heroes like him inspire us all to come forward."

Major Tandon retorted, "Don't raise this issue right now; it's not the right time to talk about it, and we have so much work to do."

All three (*Major Tandon*, *Major Romeo*, and *Major Yogi*) departed from college for home by bicycle.

Major Tandon said, "But *Cadet Charlie*'s question was right: why do soldiers and their families have to make sacrifices?"

Major Yogi confidently retorted, "No, it's not a question of sacrifice; in fact, it's a great opportunity for a soldier to serve his country."

Major Tandon asked him again, "But who will benefit from this?"

Yogi responded, "Of course, the country."

Major Romeo said it with grief. "But the key question is, who will lose?"

He answered them in the manner of inquiry: "Mother? wife? children? family? *Major Romeo*'s voice was filled with sorrow as he raised the crucial question, "Who will bear the burden of these sacrifices?" *Major Yogi* paused for a moment and replied, "It is true that soldiers and their families bear the sorrow of freedom for all of us."

The discussion ended without any conclusion and the next day we saw the entire city at the funeral of India's great son, and everyone got emotional. All of us were seated in the truck, and our truck was in the middle of a long gathering. The atmosphere was heavy with grief as we witnessed the outpouring of love and respect for the fallen soldier. People from all walks of life came together to pay their last respects, highlighting the profound impact that soldiers have on our nation's unity and collective spirit. It was a poignant reminder of the immense sacrifices made by these brave fighters and their families, reminding us that their service extends far beyond the battlefield. Additionally, we also witnessed lengthy speeches, patriotic songs, and flowers blooming along the road, but the question of "Who will lose?" remains unanswered. We were looking for answers in the tears of wife and children, the grief of parents, and, finally, the body of a martyr.

One month later,

We were returning from Kerala and waiting for the train in the waiting room at the railway station. Our train was two hours late, but we had a 50-hour journey ahead of us, so we were not too concerned. We were spread all over the places in the waiting room; some of us were sleeping on the large carpet, while others were wandering on the station. *Major Romeo* and *Major Tandon* were playing chess, and the interested cadets were divided into two groups.

Suddenly, *Major Tandon* said, "I believe this move will determine the destiny of your rook."

"Not only the future of Rook but also the future of your game," *Major Yogi* stated.

"But why is this game so complex? I don't understand how you anticipate the game so well before the move." *Santri* replied.

"Why are you anticipating?" *Major Romeo* replied. "Just look at the game and enjoy it."

"I don't like watching this game," *Santri* replied.

"Then do you want to play this game?" *Major Tandon* said.

"No, I don't know how to play it," *Santri* replied.

"Then just keep your mouth shut," *Major Tandon* replied angrily to *Santri*.

After a brief pause, *Major Yogi* responded quietly to *Santri*, "Don't worry, you can also learn this game very easily." He further added pointing to the chess board, "This chess board is like a battlefield and these pawns are the same as soldiers but unfortunately, there is no *Santri* in this company, they all play an active part in the combat." A roar of laughter filled the waiting room at *Major Yogi*'s crushing words.

Unexpectedly, three military personnel, two soldiers, and an officer entered the lobby. We didn't pay attention to him at first, but as we saw that he was the CO of our camp, we all turned to respect him. At one stroke, CO Saab inspected the train's information on the television display. We were previously informed that our train would be late, so we were ignoring the announcements. However, a sense of discipline pervaded the cadets, and the game was not going well as CO Saab entered the waiting area. Both parties were completely focused on the game and paid close attention to it without any giggles.

Both army soldiers put CO *Saab's* bags near the chair next to us and stood near the chessboard. We were surprised to see *Colonel Saab* and he was also approaching us from behind and standing close to the troops. The cadets immediately straightened their posture and saluted CO Saab, recognizing the seriousness of the situation. It was clear that his presence demanded respect and attention, causing a hushed silence to fall over the room. We encouraged *Colonel Saab* to play with us, and *Colonel Saab* readily agreed. The old game was immediately discarded, and the fresh game was ready for *Colonel Saab*. As we started the new game, *Colonel Saab*'s competitive spirit showed through, and he effortlessly showcased his strategic skills.

Our preparation was nearly complete, and we were eager to battle with *Colonel Saab*. *Major Tandon* was our commander in battling with *Colonel Saab*. The cadets were in awe of his prowess, their admiration for him growing with each move he made. It was a humbling experience to witness the Colonel's expertise firsthand, and we knew that playing with him would be an unforgettable opportunity. Nobody recognized what happened in that split second, but as soon as *Colonel Saab* noticed the cadets, they all gathered behind *Major Tandon*, and the two soldiers were stationed behind *Colonel Saab*.

The cadets eagerly awaited their turn to play alongside *Colonel Saab*, hoping to learn from his strategic genius. *Major Tandon*, now leading the group, felt a surge of responsibility and determination as he prepared to face opponents. On the other hand, *Colonel Saab* recognized the situation of polarization and realized that this match wouldn't be as simple as they were thinking; it would be a battle of cadets vs. army. He knew that the cadets proved themselves and showed their worth against the experienced army officer. *Colonel Saab* decided to observe and guide them from the sidelines, ready to step in if necessary but also allowing them the opportunity to showcase their skills.

Colonel Saab asked *Major Tandon*, "Do you know all the rules and regulations of the game?"

Major Tandon tilted his head and said, yes, sir.

Colonel Saab asked again, what is your name?

Major Tandon reveals his name in a shy manner.

"Do you know this game resembles a battlefield?" *Colonel Saab* said, and he advanced one pawn on the chessboard by saying, "And this is my brave soldier."

Major Tandon moved his pawn to the same as Colonel Saab's moved and his next three to four moves were identical to what Colonel Saab had done.

Colonel Saab commented that "your movement is similar to the army's mirror deployment." Further, he added, "You are aware of this? It's a military tactic that is likely to awe the opponent. In this mirror deployment, we increase our soldiers and military equipment to resemble the opponent. "

Major Tandon said, "It is impressive, sir."

Colonel Saab abruptly inquired, "To which unit do you belong?"

All of us said it with pride: "Artillery Unit, sir."

"So, my dear artillery warriors," *Colonel Saab* responded, "I belong to the tank unit, and this rook represents the tank on this chess board." And he moved the rook.

On the next turn, *Major Tandon* unexpectedly eliminated the rook with his bishop and stated, "Sir, your tank is stuck in the mud and not in use."

Colonel Saab responded sadly, "Of course, I like the rook in terms of heavy armor, but next time I will tell you first if I eliminate any piece of your extent. Now, you guard your bishop he is in trouble."

The next four to five moves of the game were extremely bloody, and both players eliminated more than half of the dozens of pieces.

Major Tandon impulsively said, "Sir, now your king is in danger and facing the check."

Colonel Saab responded quickly, "No problem, my brave soldier will save the king," and then he placed the pawn between the two black and white pieces."

Major Romeo asked *Colonel Saab* honestly, "Why is it that every time a soldier sacrifices his life in the service of the king?"

Colonel Saab replied calmly with a smile, "A soldier never makes a sacrifice; he always performs his duty."

"What duty are you talking about, to save the king?" *Major Yogi* asked, trembling in anger.

Colonel Saab replied, "No, not always to protect the king, but also to save his motherland, battle with the enemy to save innocent civilians, and, last but not least, to follow the order."

In the next move, *Major Tandon* eliminated the pawn defending the king and placed it in the box, and *Major Yogi* asked, "What remains after the death of the soldier?"

"A soldier is not an individual man; it is a spirit; if you kill one, the other will take over." *Colonel Saab* placed another pawn in front of the king to guard.

"So, it's endless," *Major Yogi* said.

Colonel Saab: Yes, one goes out, and the other will come in to do his job.

Major Yogi: But it's an exploitation of a soldier's duty and sacrifices.

Colonel Saab: "No, as I previously stated, a soldier is a spirit, not a job."

During this discussion, we were in a checkmate situation. We had no further moves, so *Colonel Saab* extended his hand for a victory handshake. *Major Tandon* packed everything in the box after the handshake. Suddenly, *Colonel Saab* was unexpectedly mentioned. "My dear, everyone will be sealed up in the same box, whether king or pawn, but the spirit separates us, and a spirit like a soldier not only gives us a courageous and colourful lifestyle but also a colourful coffin."

Suddenly, a train arrived on the nearby platform, and the intense noise of the train siren interrupted the conversation. Amid the chaos, *Colonel Saab* was ready with his belongings to embark on his journey.

Story 6

The Missing Bullet

The story of a bullet and how it can do damage

The firing range was the most attractive place for us, and we were delighted by the appearance of the gun. However, there were a few guidelines and rules to be followed on the firing range, and we strictly adhered to them for the sake of everyone's safety.

It was the incident at the firing range where guns were getting cleaned when suddenly, an army soldier famous as *Ali* shouted at a cadet and said, "Why did you point the gun at the other cadet? Are you stupid? This is a firing range, not a movie where you shoot like *Rambo*.

Cadet Rambo: "Sorry, sir."

(This incident made the cadet famous as Cadet Rambo throughout the NCC training.)

Ali felt angry due to the incident and told *Cadet Rambo*, "No, sorry, the Army has some discipline; you will get the punishment for this action; the gun is only directed towards the enemy, not towards your friends."

Cadet Rambo: "But, sir, this gun is empty."

Ali said, "Whatever, empty or loaded, you are not allowed to point the firearm at your friends. You know what a gun can do; do you realize how much harm a bullet can do?"

Ali stopped for a moment, and he also added, "Of course, every bullet has a target, but we're here for target practice, not to kill anyone, and as soldiers, we kill enemies, not friends. When we kill with a gun, it is not like a normal criminal killing; we, the soldiers, kill with dignity and for the discipline of our nation. Without a doubt, you will be punished, and you will be punished with a gun."

Ali further said, "Lift a gun, put it on your shoulder, and run one round of this range."

Cadet Rambo saluted *Ali* like an obedient soldier and began running through the range as instructed.

Sargeant Mohammad Ali was a wise soldier who sometimes talked like a philosopher and taught us several significant things about the war. We favoured *Ali* because of his friendly behaviour toward cadets.

Ali questioned the group, "What is a gun?"

Major Tandon instantly said, "A gun is a weapon that is used to shoot the enemy."

"Yeah, I know," *Ali* responded with a smile, "but how significant is it?"

Santri replied, "It is very important, sir."

Ali laughed and said, "Who will save you on the battlefield, either a gun or God?"

The responses of the cadets were diverse; some of them chose guns, and others chose God. Once again, *Ali* posed the question to the cadets, "Who will kill the enemy on the battlefield, we or a god?"

Ali's juggling questions dispersed the cadets' responses once more. Finally, *Ali* resolved all the confusion conveyed a philosophical standpoint, and said, "That's why, my dear cadets, you cannot distinguish between God and the gun on the battlefield." *Ali* picked up a gun from a cadet who was cleaning it and said, "Take care of it as a friend and worship it like a god."

Amid the discussions, *Cadet Rambo* appeared after punishment, saluted the Hawaladar, and rejoined the troop.

Ali further clarified, "We only cleaned the gun today, and the next day we'll practice the shooting in the lying position."

They all cleaned the gun by staying up all day and when *Major Romeo* was returning to the camp with *Cadet Rambo*, he inquired, "You don't know the code and conduct of the firing range?"

Cadet Rambo gently replied, "Yes, sir, I know, but when I suddenly saw the gun, I lost track of the code of conduct, but that gun was empty."

Major Romeo: However, it will be filled someday.

Cadet Rambo: But sir, that day I will be attentive.

Major Romeo: Yes, I understand, but as *Ali* had already clarified the guns and the enemy are the deadliest combination in the world. That's why army personnel must be disciplined.

Cadet Rambo: Oh Yes, that's why we get a heavy warm-up before touching the gun.

Major Romeo: To check your attention.

Cadet Rambo: Sometimes twice.

Major Romeo: To increase your focus.

Cadet Rambo: "Sir, I was very excited to shoot a gun, that's why I lost my temper and got punishment, but sir, I have a large collection of guns."

Major Romeo smiled and said, "The very next day, all your dreams will come true. Tomorrow we will start fresh."

The next day, the troop appeared at the firing range and was excited to shoot.

Ali explained safety protocols and stressed their importance. He ensured that each cadet understood the potential dangers associated with mishandling firearms and encouraged them to approach the training with a focused and disciplined mindset.

Ali said in a provocative tone, "Cadets, ammunition has arrived, and we will fire the guns at the targets; however, keep in mind that the ammunition is precious; so, don't waste it."

"Yes, sir," said all the cadets unanimously.

Ali: "Anybody knows the motto of the Indian Army."

'Ek Goli, Ek Dushman,' one senior cadet responded quickly.

"Yes, my cadets, in our country ammunition is limited, but our enemies are numerous, so every bullet counts," *Ali* exclaimed proudly.

Colonel Saab appeared unexpectedly, and the tent had already been set up on the firing range for him, but he approached us directly and said, "Today's firing practice will be like a competition; we'll give each cadet 10 bullets and count the marks on the target. The top scorer will receive a prize. Are you ready, boys?"

Cadets unanimously said, "Yes, sir."

The firearms had already been cleaned and were ready to use. The cadets eagerly lined up; their eyes fixed on the targets ahead. There were also two other groups of cadets refilling the magazine with bullets. The first ten cadets were chosen for target practice, and the next ten for shell collection. The chosen cadets were writing their names and enrolment numbers on the target paper before affixing it to the practice board.

To operate self-loading rifles (SLR) in the range, two cadets are required, one is in the firing position, and the other is to assist the first cadet in collecting or stopping the casing by his cap. Luckily, I and *Cadet Rambo* were both together on that day; I was in the laying position, and he was my shell collector for firing practice. We were both waiting for instructions and aware of the orders issued by army officers. *Cadet Rambo* was on the firing range for the first time, so he was unaware of the huge noise of shooting into the firing range; I was accustomed to it.

Without any warning, I heard the word "fire," and we all immediately started shooting while a deafening roar of fire was all around the range. *Cadet Rambo* was becoming uneasy due to the loud noise of the SLR (self-loading rifle), but he was unable to act because his hands were busy collecting the casing by the cap. After a while, the noise died down, and all ten cadets finished their magazines and were waiting for the next order. The following instructions were to

Finish all the fire.

Unload the magazine.

Double cock the gun.

Fire once again.

Leave the gun and stand up.

Check the target.

I dashed to check my target, and I noticed *Cadet Rambo* behind me counting the 10 bullet cases and scratching his ear.

When I returned, he hurriedly asked me, "What's the score? How much is in the bull?"

"Five inside the bull, the rest outside," I replied quickly.

"Bullet cases have completely counted." I inquired.

"All have been counted and submitted to the account," *Cadet Rambo* replied.

"Great job! Let's head back to the shooting range and prepare for the next round," I suggested.

The shooting continued till the drink break. The flags behind the target continuously display the wind direction and pressure. On the other hand, *Colonel Saab* was calmly counting each cadet's points on the judgment sheet beneath the tent. As usual, army personnel were instructing the other cadets to take a deep breath, set the target, and fire. *Cadet Rambo* finally got his chance to fire and thoroughly enjoyed it.

However, a cadet reported that a bullet was missing from the record. The firing practice was instantly halted, and everyone focused on this matter. After a long search for bullets inside the truck and on the firing range, we came up empty-handed. We organized ourselves into an orderly formation, and then *Ali* said, "I hope you all understand the importance of a bullet; every bullet has a desired target, and I hope this missing bullet's target is not a person but a practice board."

When he was talking about the lost bullet, he became personal, and *Colonel Saab* saw Ali's face. *Ali* roared again and instructed us, "We will divide into three groups, each with ten members, and investigate every inch of this firing range until we get the bullet."

After two hours of hard work, we found the missing bullet. *Colonel Saab* was happy to see the cadets' hard work and appreciated it. He commended *Ali* for his leadership and determination in organizing the search effort. The successful recovery of the missing bullet restored a sense of accomplishment and pride among the cadets, reaffirming their commitment to excellence in their training.

We hurriedly packed up all the equipment and guns. As we loaded everything into the trucks, *Colonel Saab* reminded us to always prioritize safety and the proper handling of firearms. He emphasized the importance of regular maintenance and inspections to prevent any future mishaps. The evening progressively intensified like a stupor, and the flags fell fast as if someone had taken his revenge.

Colonel Saab disclosed the result, and *Mr. Sniper*, a cadet, received the highest marks in the competition. With a hero's welcome, we all applaud him. *Ali* also revealed to the squad an important fact: *Mr. Sniper's* father is also in the army and served in the infantry division. He also added that my father was also a soldier in the infantry division, and his battalion was stationed in Kashmir when he sacrificed his life.

Following all of this, we clapped with great discipline. We were all overjoyed because our wish to shoot had come true. When *Colonel Saab* was about to leave, I saw they were both talking about something, and I believe *Ali* was confirming the year of his father's death and indicating the gunshot marks on his father's body.

Ali got back into the truck after his conversation with *Colonel Saab*, and our truck drove towards home. *Colonel Saab's* car was the first to move down the dusty road in our queue of trucks. The entire road was coated in dust.

Story 7

The Worn Tank

The story of JCO Subedar Mammad Singh

To appear in the NCC B and C certificate examination, cadets must have completed at least two training camps. After the first camp, we were terrified, so we had no interest in attending anymore. On the other hand, our seniors had moved on and were busy with their lives. We had become the seniors of our unit. When newly recruited cadets saluted, it filled us with pride and glory. Surprisingly One day, our ANO, Lieutenant AB, ordered us to attend the MHOW camp. We were perplexed because we couldn't deny the order, and the Mhow was already the military headquarters of war. We were terrified because that camp would turn into the full movie that we saw at the first camp. But ultimately, we packed our belongings once more, boarded the train, and travelled to Mhow.

At the Mhow railway station, we observed army trainee troops and officers. The stars on their shoulders were twinkling, and their uniform was gleaming with pride. We were looking forward to experiencing the army campus, training program, and weaponry. On the other hand, outside the railway station, a powerful army truck decorated with green camouflage was waiting for us. We all piled into the truck, and it entered the restricted army area. We were impressed to see the big guns and mortars displayed in front of various battalion offices. The soldiers were busy with their duties, and their disciplined movements and sharp salutes reflected their commitment. Inside the army truck, *Santri* was feeling nervous to see the healthy army man and told *Major Romeo*, "I think this camp is also going to be as hardworking as the previous one."

Major Tandon replied humorously, "Why are you worried? You can become the *Santri* once again."

Santri replied modestly "I am *Santri* by accident, not by choice, and *Santri* also has some guarding duties. When you go on parade, I protect your belongings, and when you return from your hard work, I arrange the water and tea for you."

Major Tandon responded, "That means you will become a *Santri* in this camp as well."

Santri answered, "No, I wanted to do the parade and fire the guns, but I'm unable to do the hard work due to illness."

The fighting continued until we arrived at the campsite. As we approached the campsite, we realized that the present camp would be different than what we had before. The campus was lush, and the daytime breeze was pleasant, but there was barbed wire fencing covering the entire area. In the evening roll call, when the cadets were arranged properly, *Major Tandon* stood in the last row of N-threes and whispered, "Welcome to the Central Jail."

Suddenly, the roll call procedure started, and SUOs from various units started handing over their cadet counts to the camp senior. The camp senior presented the detailed report to a half-aged Army officer saying, "300 cadets from 11 different battalions are present, sir," said Camp Senior.

In response, the half-aged army man said loudly, "Relex, cadets.". He addressed the gathering, and every cadet was attentively listening to his speech. The stars were shining on his shoulder, and a baton was in his hand. He explained, “Cadets, this place resembles a fort, and I am the premier of this place, Subedar Mammad Singh. For the next ten days, you will be under my supervision, and I will teach you the various military tactics of the Indian army and the Sikh regiments. You will also see a real battlefield, gun practice, and a war plan.”

All cadets remained attentive in N-threes formation as *Subedar Saab* inspected each one. Cadets had also examined his uniform, posture, and determination while he was inspecting. Suddenly he warned sternly, “Remember, discipline is the backbone of this camp. Any violation will be treated seriously.”

The cadets exchanged glances, realizing the gravity of the situation they were about to face. *Subedar Saab* turned around and walked towards the other group of cadets on the ground. I noticed an issue with his one leg, as he was physically incapable of running. Despite his physical limitations, he commanded respect and authority among the cadets. His experience and knowledge were evident in the way he spoke and carried himself.

Subedar Saab addressed “Dear cadets here you’ll feel like you’re in a real military training camp, and don't try to become smart or bunk because my spy is everywhere in the camp."

He further said, pointing towards a device mounted on the roof of the officer's mess, "You will obey all orders and directions conveyed through this loudspeaker. Any Doubt?"

"No, sir!" said all the cadets loudly.

Subedar Saab said again, "Any questions?"

"No, sir," said the whole battalion with a higher pitch.

The roll call ended without any question, and we finished our dinner immediately because we were too exhausted from the long journey. Since we were stationed so close to the regular army, the food was of very high quality. We were aware that a challenging PT session was scheduled for early in the morning, so we went to bed early.

But roughly around 2.00 AM at midnight, a terrifying alarm went off and awakened all the cadets in camp, including myself. I tried to reassure myself that the alarm had not accidentally gone off, but we quickly realized that it was a call for an emergency drill. That was my first experience with an emergency drill, and I'm sure it was the first for every cadet in the camp. Some cadets were terrified and started obeying the instructions given by

Subedar Saab. We were in a dilemma about whether to follow the instructions or refuse. On the other hand, *Subedar Saab* continuously announced over the loudspeakers, "All cadets must be present in full uniform on the ground within ten minutes. Those who come after 10 minutes or without proper uniforms will receive punishment."

All the cadets were complying with orders and preparing themselves to deploy to the parade ground. There was very little time left to gather and some of the junior cadets of my team had already gathered on the parade ground in full uniform. On the contrary, it was quite difficult to find your shoes and uniform at night, so everyone was in haste. Some cadets were struggling to locate their belongings in the darkness, causing a sense of urgency and panic. Others were helping each other by shining flashlights and calling out to one another, fostering a spirit of cooperation amidst the chaos.

On the other hand, we had opposite views. We were thinking that 'the whole practice is for scaring the cadets'. We had assumed that *Subedar Saab* wouldn't find the cadets improperly uniformed, and the punishment would be limited to threatening the cadets. We approached the ground dressed inappropriately and without shoes within the time limit. We were all sleepy, and we anticipated that *Subedar Saab* wouldn't be able to check all the 300 cadets at midnight, but all our predictions were going wrong on that day. He inspected all the cadets, and only we two were dressed inappropriately.

In the dark night, we were both waiting for the punishment, and *Subedar Saab* stood in front of us. He separated us from the gathering and explained to the cadets: "You must be attentive as a soldier; you cannot make excuses or violate instructions in the army. It's a part of training, and on the battlefield during the war, it will help you."

He also added, "During the Kargil war, I was on the border. If the sirens went off, we were ready to move at any time. As I've already said, you will get better training here."

Subedar Saab turned around and explained to us, "Remember one thing; the second name of discipline is *Subedar Mammad Singh*."

Subedar Saab finished the roll call, and the cadets proceeded to their tent. We were both left there and waiting for the punishment. We were thinking about the different kinds of punishments, like crawling and dips, but we both only got night duty outside *Subedar Saab*'s tent for the entire camp.

Our routine had been fixed since that night, and we both felt like *Subedar Saab*'s personal assistants. Throughout the camp, we served him tea, assembled food thali from the canteen, and guarded the camp until he fell asleep. We also occasionally went to the vegetable market with *Subedar Saab* to buy vegetables for the camp, and sometimes we used the loudspeaker to announce important information to the cadets. In our spare time, we speculated whether this was a punishment or a retest of the camp's hurdle. However, that camp was not as challenging as we expected. During the day, we spent some time in the lecture hall listening to the lectures on war history or in the small firing range. The small firing range was very close to the campsite where we practiced with point 22 (0.22) rifle. The .22 was the neck diameter of that Rifle but our instructor called it *Chidi maar Rifle*.

One morning in the camp, we were excited to be wearing our uniforms because we were going to the big firing range to ride in a tank. It was an exciting opportunity for us to experience the power and control of a tank. We were both extremely thrilled and secured our positions outside the *Subedar Saab* tent, as usual. *Subedar Saab* arrived with his artillery uniform and big cap. We all piled into the truck after lunch and were stationed at a large firing range. As we approached the firing range, we did not see any tanks but rather a tent with food set up. We were perplexed that the plan had changed. However, our excitement quickly turned to disappointment as we realized that our training session had been cancelled due to unforeseen circumstances.

Inside the truck, *Santri* told *Major Tandon* after seeing the food setup at the firing range, "I think a heavy breakfast is planned for us."

"Fool, this isn't for us; we've already eaten," *Major Tandon* retorted.

"I assume some soldiers' company is coming here for certain tasks," *Major Yogi* answered.

Major Romeo replied, "But where is the tank?"

Major Tandon said abruptly, "Oh, our truck is parked in the wrong location; look at there, *Subedar Saab* is waiting for us outside the creek."

We all crossed the empty creek and reunited with other members of our camp. As we settled under the shade of the tree, *Subedar Saab* said, "Boys, as you all know, we have two jobs here: first to view the vital exercise 'Missile Milap' and then to ride the tank," directing his batons towards the tank, which was positioned very far into the ground. We were all curious about both things; some cadets wanted to view the rehearsal of 'Missile Milap' while others wished to ride in the tank. However, *Subedar Saab* responded first about the Missile Milap: "Cadets, the Missile Milap is a Russian-made anti-tank missile that chases and destroys the target." He further clarified, "With a normal anti-tank gun, we can't guide the missile, but with this missile, we can chase after the fire."

He further added, pointing to a location within the shooting range, "You can see some sort of movable target arrangement there."

Suddenly, a cadet inquired, "When will we get a chance to tank ride?"

"The tank takes some time to start, so after all these activities, we will ride the tank" *Subedar Saab* replied.

Soldiers continued firing Missile Milap throughout the day with varying degrees of success (some missiles hit the target, others didn't). To help the army officer, some of the selected cadets were given the chance to fire the missile. When the missile successfully hit the target, all the cadets rejoiced. At the same time, we were waiting for the tank ride, anticipating that it would be a thrilling experience after witnessing the successful missile strikes.

After target practice till the evening, we got the chance to ride in the tank. We all ran for the tank on the ground, and some cadets were able to sit inside the tank while others were on top of it. The cadets were filled with anticipation as they climbed into the tank, excited to feel the power and energy of being inside such a formidable machine. We both fell behind in the race to sit on the tank.

Major Romeo told *Major Yogi*, who stood near the *Subedar Saab*, "I think this tank has retired from the army."

Abruptly, *Subedar Saab* answered *Major Romeo*'s question, "Of course, this was a fighter tank and played a significant role in the 1971 battle, but now it is used to entertain the children. You can see the dent and bullet mark on its armour."

The other cadets were moving around the tank, and army soldiers were expelling them to touch the barrel. The driver was trying to start the engine of the tank and the soldiers were afraid about the safety of the cadets and wanted to prevent any accidents. After some time, *Subedar Saab* provided some instructions to the driver, but the tank didn't start for another hour. The evening was becoming darker, and the tank wasn't ready to start, so *Subedar Saab* abandoned the plan and promised to ride on the tank some other day. We were all sad because the tank's engine did not start, and we were hoping for the best to ride in the tank.

In the next few days, nothing new happened, and we were both doing our duty outside the *Subedar Saab* tent as usual. *Subedar Saab*'s routine was straightforward; around 2000 hrs, Swamy (the cook) placed the plate inside the tent, and he finished his meal by 2030 hrs. We also knew that *Subedar Saab* occasionally swallowed any prescribed red solution before his meal. But one day, we noticed that *Subedar Saab* did not finish his meal till 2100 hrs, and their friends were pacifying him. However, the hustle was too much on that day, and many friends and army personnel were arriving at night.

We didn't have the authority to look inside the tent, so we stood outside, waiting for the *Subedar Saab* to fall asleep and the lights to be turned off. Around 2200 hrs, Swamy arrived and collected the plates, turned off the lights, then sat outside the tent with us and quietly said, "Family is very important."

We both sit on the drum near Swamy and move our heads to say yes. Swamy was a cheerful, happy man who joyfully prepared food for the cadets. Swami pulled out a cigar case and spent some time identifying the appropriate cigarette. After identifying the perfect cigarette, Swamy lit it up and took a deep breath. While exhaling smoke into the air, he advised us, "The life of a soldier is quite difficult; it requires dedication, and gradually you adopt that lifestyle and start loving it. At the same time, your family needs your assistance, and this great quandary demands an excellent balance of work and family.

He took another deep breath and said, "But sometimes problems and disagreements win when a soldier loses. We've been part of *Subedar Saab*'s family for the past ten years, and they've treated us like his own kids. But what will happen when he retires? He doesn't want to go back to his lonely house."

In the end, he dragged the final breath of the cigarette, threw it far off, and told us, "One day this job will be over, but your family will always be with you." He stood by his chair, scolded both of us for wasting our time, and ordered us to head back to the tent.

The next day, we got the opportunity to enjoy a ride in the tank, but we both preferred to sit inside the tank.

Story 8

Washing Allowance

The story of experiencing patriotism

After a year of selfless service, our ANO unexpectedly informed us about the provision of a washing allowance. We were happy to hear that we would receive large sums of money in the form of a washing allowance. This surprising news brought a wave of excitement among all the cadets, as it was a recognition of our hard work and dedication. The washing allowance would provide financial relief and motivate us to do our best in our duties. We were eager to learn how this allowance would be distributed. However, we knew that obtaining government funds was like squeezing water from a stone. There were certain procedures and paperwork needed to get the washing allowance. The cadets were informed about the necessary steps needed to take, such as filling out forms and attaching relevant documentation, etc.; additionally, the cadets should have patience.

We gathered at the battalion office after the parade with a big form that required lots of signatures and verification.

Major Tandon told to *Major Romeo* after seeing that lengthy form, "I don't think this form will be filled today."

Major Romeo: "Not today, but it will be filled in this week."

Major Tandon: "Yes, because it needed the signature of our ANO for attendance verification, then the college principal, and then it will be submitted to the battalion officer."

Major Yogi: Yes, it is a more complicated process than property transfers.

Major Romeo: legally?

Major Yogi: Of course, legally; otherwise, illegally, you don't require any document.

Major Tandon: How much money will we get from this lengthy process?

Major Yogi: This money will be sufficient for 20 *samosas*.

Major Tandon: Only 20 *samosas*; why are we doing such hard work for this amount?

Major Romeo interrupted the discussion and said, "Because it is our right."

Major Yogi: Of course, money is not so important, but it is our right and a recognition of our hard work too.

The conversation continued until we arrived at the movie theatre, where we frequently spent our evenings. We were enjoying ourselves outside the theatre and waiting for entry into the movie hall.

Major Yogi: What is the reason for the low crowd in this movie?

Major Romeo: People are not showing their interest in watching this movie.

Major Yogi: So, why are we here?

Major Romeo: Because we are different and have come here to give tribute to the ultimate soldier, '*Bose, the forgotten hero*'.

Major Yogi: Oh, I forgot to tell you.

Major Romeo: What?

Major Yogi: Your name is on the short attendance list in the practical lab.

Major Romeo: Yes, I know.

Abruptly, *Major Tandon* said to the group, I think the door of the cinema hall has opened.

Major Yogi: Oh yes, now we can enter the hall.

They all vanished into the darkness of the cinema hall, lost in the enjoyment of reel life.

The next day, we all approached the ANO office to verify our attendance. *Captain AB* was delighted to see us all together and shared one piece of information with us by saying, "Cadets, every year on December 7, the Indian Army celebrates Armed Forces Flag Day and organizes a fundraising campaign to honor the martyrs and the man in uniform who valiantly fought and continue to fight on our borders to safeguard the country's honour. This year, we will raise funds for affected soldiers of the Kargil War. Suddenly, he asked, do you know about the Kargil War?"

Major Romeo replied hurriedly: Yes, sir, I have watched the movie.

Captain AB said regretfully, "The actual war was far more bitter than the movie. Thousands of soldiers lost their lives, and many were disabled in that war. Dear cadets, our efforts will be a small contribution from our side to help soldiers and their families. In this campaign, we will raise money by selling Armed Forces Flag Day tickets. The price of the tickets is 5, 10, or 50 rupees, and our battalion has set some targets for our unit, but I am sure we will break the target. Are you ready, boys?"

All the cadets said unanimously, 'Yes, sir.'

Captain AB: I am giving this responsibility to *Sergeant Romeo*, and you will work under his leadership.

All the cadets roared again, 'Yes, sir.'

We got back to our work immediately after the meeting. We decided to divide ourselves into two small groups and planned to reach out to every person on the college premises. *Major Romeo* and *Major Tandon* were members of Group 1, while

Major Yogi and a few junior cadets were members of Group 2. Two hours later, we gathered at the parade ground and sat under the national flag, which was situated in front of the main building.

Major Romeo asked *Major Yogi*, "What are the people's responses?"

Major Yogi responded sluggishly, "Mixed; some of them are convinced, and some flatly refused to buy tickets."

Major Romeo: So why are you upset? Don't worry; we will find the perfect hand for these tickets.

Major Yogi: No, I am not worried about the tickets; it will find the appropriate hand. But why do people need explanations?

Major Romeo: What happened? Tell me overtly.

Major Yogi: Why are people not interested in purchasing these tickets? After all, we are not doing anything wrong.

Major Romeo: Because they don't know the significance of these tickets.

Major Tandon: I think people are unaware of soldiers' sacrifices.

Major Yogi: No, I disagree with your viewpoint. People are aware of soldiers' sacrifices, but they do not wish to recognize or support them. Their priorities are comfort and entertainment rather than honouring those who serve our country.

Major Romeo: But tickets are not so costly.

Major Tandon posed a philosophical question to *Major Romeo*: "Yes, tickets are not so expensive, but what is the true price of soldiers' sacrifices?"

Major Yogi smiled and said, yes, it's a wonderful time to pose this fantastic question.

Major Romeo: I think at least people should recognize their sacrifices.

Major Tandon: Recognition's fine, but my question remains unanswered: What is the true price of soldiers' sacrifices?

A junior cadet named *Lieutenant Jack* suddenly entered the conversation and said to the group, "Sir, I visited a war memorial and I think that's true respect and recognition for the soldiers and their sacrifices.

Major Tandon replied, "I agree; this is a positive initiative, but my question remains answered."

Lieutenant Jack: Sir, please forget the question for a second, but there, we can also see how beautifully a gun represents a soldier.

Major Romeo: A 'Rifle' is only the thing that can represent the soldiers.

"The Material of the 'Rifle' is the unbroken courage of a soldier and the Bullets" *Major Yogi* paused for a moment and said, "Bullets are the spirit."

Major Romeo: A fiery spirit.

Major Tandon: Absolutely, A Rifle can justify the soldier's attributes and spirit. But 'What is the true cost of soldiers' respect?'

Major Yogi: For your question, we may seek the help of an expert.

Major Romeo: But now it is time to go back home.

Major Yogi: All right. Tomorrow, we'll start a new day of our campaign with new energy.

Major Tandon: Of course, because we forgot to get the signature of ANO, sir, on the washing allowance form.

The evening was becoming softer as the sun began to set. The group packed their belongings and headed back to their homes. The next day, we received the same mixed response as yesterday. We shared our experience with our ANO, and he suggested that we should plan our campaign outside the campus as well. He believed that reaching out to people beyond the campus would help us extend our reach and add more support for our cause. He also suggested that you should wear uniforms to encourage a sense of commitment and perseverance in society, and we all agreed to an off-campus campaign.

In the upcoming days, we diligently carried out campaigns off-campus, and uniforms imparted magic to that campaign. We sold out all the tickets, and the people were incredibly encouraging of our cause. The sight of a group of uniformed cadets advocating for a meaningful campaign seemed to resonate with the community. We not only raised sufficient funds, but we also sparked conversations and spread awareness in the nearby society. During the campaign, we took all the required signatures on the washing allowance form and submitted it to the battalion office.

One day, suddenly, we got a message from the battalion office, and we were happy to be rewarded for our hard work in terms of washing allowance. Of course, it was a small amount, but it meant a lot to us as cadets. We had already planned how we would spend this money. Perhaps some of us wanted to treat ourselves to tasty food or buy something, which we had been demanding for a while. In contrast, others had decided to save the money for future expenditures. However, on the same day, our ANO encouraged us to contribute to Armed Forces Flag Day as cadets.

The cadets gave a mixed response to contributing to this campaign. Some cadets expressed enthusiasm and agreed with *Captain AB*, recognizing the importance of supporting our armed forces, but others looked hesitant, questioning 'how their small contributions can make a significant impact.'

Captain AB stated, "Yes, I know you're not earning any money and have a lot of liabilities as a student, but despite these limitations, I will recommend you contribute. I will not force you to contribute a significant amount, but you should." He also added: To demonstrate unity, I placed a box inside the office where you can go one by one and contribute your amount.

After some hesitation, finally, all the cadets agreed with this new arrangement and showed their willingness to contribute. Cadets entered the office one by one and made their contributions to the campaign. The parade concluded, and some of the groups were conversing and revealing their amounts to their friends, while others were concealing them. The evening was getting darker, and the cadets were leaving the college grounds like flocks of birds in the sky. *Major Tandon*, *Major Romeo*, and *Major Yogi* cancelled their plan to watch the movie and headed home.

Major Tandon abruptly said to the group, "Today, I also got the answer to my question."

Major Yogi: Which question?

Major Tandon replied, what is the true price of soldiers' sacrifices?

Major Romeo: What answer do you get?

Major Tandon replied philosophically: "The true price of soldier sacrifices is always stayed inside you. You will never find the answer outside."

Lieutenant Jack innocently said, "No, I do not understand. Please explain."

Major Tandon: My dear Jack, in contrast to *Amar Jawan Jyoti* or Dropbox, you just reflect whatever is inside you."

Lieutenant Jack: No, I am not getting your point, sir.

Major Romeo said humbly, my dear Jack, *Major Tandon* is trying to say, 'You can't expect anything from others; just contribute your part. It is not a matter of bragging. Do you understand now?

Lieutenant Jack: Not completely.

Now *Major Yogi* ordered *Lieutenant Jack* to come forward in the bicycle lane and tried to explain to him by saying, "How much money have you contributed?"

Lieutenant Jack was about to speak, but *Major Romeo* stopped him in the middle and said, "Don't share, just say how much money you have contributed. Just say yes if you contributed all the money in your pocket.

Lieutenant Jack replied horridly, No.

Major Yogi: Why not all the money?

Lieutenant Jack: Because the rest of the money is for my other expenditures, such as fees, books, stationery, etc.

Major Yogi: So, my dear, your contribution is not a symbol of patriotism, respect, or honour inside you.

Lieutenant Jack: But today, all activities were confidential, and nobody will know my contribution until I won't reveal the truth.

Major Romeo: That's why everyone knows his contribution deep inside the heart, opposite the mirror. Patriotism is an internal matter, not a matter of judgment.

Lieutenant Jack: Now I realize the true meaning of your words. Ultimately, this is not a matter of evaluating or demonstrating.

Major Romeo: Finally, I and *Captain AB* both succeeded in explaining to you.

During that conversation, we all came to a fork in the road where we had to choose a specific route to get back home.

Story 9

A Love Letter

The story of affection and tragedy

The moment in the afternoon during the camp when *Major Tandon* and *Major Romeo* were resting inside the tent.

"Major, you know in this camp only guns and bullets are female, no one else," *Major Tandon* asked *Major Romeo*.

"That's why the soldiers are so desperate about it," replied Romeo. "But why are you talking about this unexpectedly?" He added.

Major Tandon: Today I was in the kitchen for my duty, and *Mohammad Ali* and *Jagrup Singh* were both talking about *Rani*.

"Who is Rani?" *Major Romeo* inquired.

Major Tandon: "That's the point; I'm also curious about Rani and stayed there."

"Then you figured out who this Rani is?" *Major Romeo* said.

Major Tandon: "No, but she's a killer."

"And lightweight as well," Romeo added.

"Yes, but how do you know?" *Major Tandon* asked.

"Fool, it's our newly introduced rifle, *INSAS*," *Major Romeo* said.

"Then why was *Jagrup Singh* comparing it to his wife?" *Major Tandon* asked.

"Because it is capable of bursting fire," *Major Romeo* said.

"Busting fire?" *Major Tandon* inquired.

Major Romeo explained, "It can fire all bullets in a single moment."

Major Tandon: "Are you sure they weren't talking about any women?"

"Of course, there are many similarities, but I'm sure they were discussing the rifle," *Major Romeo* explained.

Major Tandon asked "One more thing I want to discuss. When I was in the kitchen *Jagrup* was telling *Ali*, 'I don't know when you'll get your queen, but our battalion is going to receive our queen with a crown today itself.' What does it mean? Can you please elaborate?"

Major Romeo: I cannot confirm this, but I believe this new gun has aiming gear resembling a crown.

"Oh, I remember the same as the LMG (Light Machine Gun)," *Major Tandon* said.

Major Tandon: "One more important thing, they were talking about any love letter."

Major Romeo amazingly said, "Love letter?"

"Yes," *Major Tandon* replied. "Next month I'll enjoy the mountains with my Rani, and you stay here with your love letter."

Major Romeo said after a brief pause, "That means *Jagrup* has a new posting, but what about the love letter?

A deep sleep interrupted this conversation, and when they woke up, the cadets were getting ready and dressed in uniforms in the back portion of the tent. They both noticed *Major AG* washing his face with an expensive face wash.

Major Romeo told to *Major AG*, "Hey, Major, why are you wasting time cleaning your face because you know that there is no girl in this camp?"

"I'm not washing my face for any girl; I don't like this wheatish face," *Major AG* responded.

"Major, correct yourself; it's not wheatish, it's blackish, and all your efforts will be wasted because you cannot be fair after using this face wash or any other cream," *Major Tandon* replied.

Major AG threw the fairness cream and dashed to catch *Major Tandon*. *Major Tandon* mostly began his days in this manner, and this type of fighting was common in the camp. *Major AG* is one of our good friends, but he is always conscious of his looks.

During the roll call, *Major Yogi* asked AG, "Hey, Major, what is the name of your girlfriend with whom you spend the most time?"

"She is not my girlfriend, fool; she is simply my friend," *Major AG* replied.

"Is there any difference between the two words?" *Major Tandon* questioned.

"When you have a girlfriend, then you will understand what the difference is; otherwise, you always figure out the same thing," *Major AG* said.

Major Romeo: "That's correct; otherwise, you can't figure out the difference between the gun and the girl."

Major Tandon smiled and positively moved his head.

"Now if you can differentiate, it means you have girlfriends as well," *Major Yogi* said.

"No, that's not the exact interpretation of my words," *Major AG* replied.

Major Yogi asked *Major AG*: "Major, tell me the truth; she likes you. What's the name of the girl you're always mentioning?"

Amazingly, *Major AG* spoke back: *PS1184*?

Major Yogi: Yes, so now you're going to tell the truth about *PS1184*.

Major AG replied, "Please stop right now; this is not the right place to discuss these issues."

Major Tandon: "We're getting stopped, but we want to hear the entire story."

Major AG: "There is no story; these are just kisses and talks about my affair."

Major Yogi: But we have always noticed a grin on your face whenever you talk about *PS1184*.

Major AG: "Friends, please keep your mouth shut and stop talking about *PS1184*. Now I am giving you a piece of secret information about the new mission, 'Operation Juliet'.

"We're on the mission; we're working on a new plan to get to the pond or bunk," *Major Tandon* replied innocently.

"No, we are not planning anything like that," *Major Romeo* replied to *Major Tandon* humbly.

Major Tandon: "So, what exactly is '*Operation Juliet?*'"

Major Romeo: It's a secret mission.

Major Tandon: "So how does *Major AG* know about your secret plan?"

Major Romeo: "Because we are both in the same coaching class and need each other to complete this plan."

"No, you're hiding something," *Major Tandon* replied.

Major AG: "Okay, I'll tell you the truth. *Major Romeo* involves me in this secret mission, '*Operation Juliet*'.

Major Tandon: What exactly is this '*Operation Juliet*'?

Major AG: "*Major Romeo* adores a girl, and my job is to puncture her scooter on a specific day."

Major Tandon: "What will be the sense of all this? She will fall in love with Romeo."

Major AG smiled and said, "No, but Romeo gets a chance to help her and spend quality time with her."

Major Tandon inquired hastily, "Every day?"

"Fool, only once," *Major Romeo* replied.

Major Romeo: But *Major Tandon*, we need your help today.

Major Tandon: For what?

Major Romeo: You were talking about some love letters in the afternoon.

Major Tandon: Yes, *Ali* has a love letter, but why are you curious about that?

Major Romeo and *Major AG* both say simultaneously, "Because we want that love letter to be read for future reference."

Major Tandon: It's not a good habit to read letters without permission.

Major AG: "Just for reference, we will never read any love letters after this."

"OK, *Major Tandon* is ready; we'll go to *Ali's* tent tonight," *Major Romeo* concluded.

The roll call ended with a resounding vote, and we all agreed to meet *Ali* inside his tent late after dinner to clear up any confusion.

After dinner, we reached *Ali's* tent and he suddenly asked us "Tell me, boys, why are you coming here late at night?"

Major Romeo: Sir, we need to know about the INSAS rifle for our upcoming B certificate test.

Ali: Oh, it's wonderful, lightweight, and completes all 20 rounds in a single push.

Major Yogi: It can fire bursts like an LMG (light machine gun).

Ali: Yes, and it's lighter than LMG, so you can carry it easily.

Romeo: Sir, may I ask you another question?"

Ali: "Why not?"

Romeo: Sir, why do you say '*Ram, Ram Saab Ji*' when you salute with a gun?

Ali: "Because it is one of the ways to salute in my battalion."

Major Tandon: But, sir, you are a Muslim.

Ali: So, what? My entire battalion salutes in this manner, and you also sing every day in your NCC song, *'Ek hi apna Ram Hai, Ek hi Allahatala hai.' (Our Gods are the same).*

Quickly, *Romeo* fired another question and inquired, "Sir, are you married?"

Ali: No, but why are you asking?

"Because *Major Tandon* fell in love," *Major Romeo* said.

"Two things are very dangerous in the world," *Ali* said in his usual philosophical tone.

"What are they, sir?" *Major Tandon* inquired rapidly.

"The first is war, and the second is love," *Ali* answered.

"Sir, I recognize the war, but why is love dangerous?" *Major Romeo* responds.

Ali responds calmly, "Because both of these things are the cause of changes."

Major AG agrees with *Ali*: "Sir, you are correct; my girlfriend insists that I change my hairstyle from the soldier cut to the Shahrukh Khan style.

Ali responds with a humorous tone, "Stop obeying her advice; otherwise, you will not pass the B certificate examination."

Major AG replied, "I understand, sir, but she always encourages me."

Major AG's innocent response impressed *Ali*: "Truly, I just received a letter from my fiancée, and she is pressuring me to come home for her birthday." How do I explain to her that I don't have a routine job; I am in the army?

"Sir, you still communicate by letter, not by telephone," *Major Romeo* said.

Ali explained, "In my opinion, I feel constrained over the telephone and can't express my thoughts freely, but on the pages, I feel liberated."

"Sir, you wanted to be a writer?" *Major Romeo* asked.

Ali quickly responded, "Not at all; I am a warrior and am proud to be a soldier."

"Sir, how do you impress your girlfriend by writing a letter?" *Major Romeo* asked.

Ali explained clearly: "Do your best to be a trustworthy person while writing the love letter. Write down your feelings and thoughts in a straightforward manner. Let me show you an example. He rose and searched in his pocket for something. He finally found his purse under the pillow and gave a piece of paper to us."

My eyes filled with joy as he opened the love letter, and I smiled to show my delight.

Suddenly, the mournful song *'Tujhe Bhulna to Chaha lekin Bhula na Paye' (A song in the melodious voice of Attaullah Khan)* played on the loudspeaker. We knew that the loudspeaker was under the supervision of *Subedar Saab*, and the mournful song in the night acted as a signal to go to bed.

Ali stopped the conversation immediately to ensure that we would not divulge any information to the public and ordered us to proceed to the tent. He blessed us by saying, *Rabba Kheriya* may you never be cheated in your life."

We left *Ali*'s tent without any delay and walked fast towards our tent to traverse the officer's tent to avoid any confrontation with *Subedar Saab*. We were accustomed to this song, and it had etched into our memory. The melody of the song gladdened us when we were passing by the *Subedar Saab* tent, and the song was continuously playing in the background.

"Allaha kare ye Dhoka, Allaha Kare ye Dhoka, tu bhi kisi se khaye...."

Story 10

Alexander The Great

The story of the negligence of duty, revolt in dreams, and arson in the armoury

It was a cozy evening in the camp; dark clouds loomed overhead, threatening to unleash a torrential downpour. The sun had set, but the sky appeared to be a large canvas on which everyone could find their creativity. The cadets often gathered around the rock and shared stories and laughter. It was a peaceful escape from the rigors of training, a moment of connection with nature amid their demanding days. The rock was a small plateau near the campsite where the cadets spent most of their time, especially in the evening. The plateau provided a serene backdrop for the cadets to unwind and recharge, allowing them to find solace in the simplicity of nature. As we observed the scorpions and crabs, we were reminded of the beauty and resilience of life.

Major Yogi told *Major Tandon* while he was sitting on the rock and throwing a stone at the target by making an aim, "I am missing my family, and I want to go home."

"Yes, I'm tired of this one-month-long camp life and night duty." *Major Tandon* was upset.

"You're both correct; we need some rest but still have fifteen days until the Republic Day parade," *Major Romeo* replied.

Major Yogi said, "Really, we all want to go to class, eat the food that our mothers have cooked, and spend time with our families, but here we are, taking food from *Shaitan Singh's* hands." He further added, "But *Subedar Shaitan Singh* is a good man, and he loves us the same as members of his family."

"But what about our family?" *Major Tandon* replied irritably.

"Of course, we are all family; we live together and spend our valuable time with each other," *Santri* said.

"But, without a doubt, the duration of this camp is excessive; I want to flee," *Major Tandon* stated.

"Don't lose hope, friends; we will all work together to finish this Republic Day parade," *Major Romeo* said. "Can you recall what *Mammad Singh* said?"

They all said it together, '*Ladenge Akhiri Saans Tak*' (We will fight till the last breath).

The night was getting dark, and everyone was flocking to the campsite.

"Does anyone have night duty tonight?" *Romeo* inquired.

Major Tandon replied, "Yes, I will be with you tonight from 0200 to 0400 hrs in the armoury near the temple area."

"With me?" *Romeo* surprised.

"Yes, you have duty tonight with me," *Major Tandon* said calmly.

Major Yogi advised *Major Tandon.* "The armoury duty is risky; you have to be attentive throughout the duty due to the importance of weapons."

"However, it is far superior to lavatory ground, which I performed last night," *Santri* stated slowly.

"Truly, the lavatory ground is a filthy place, but today I will sleep on duty hours, behind the temple, on the mattress," *Major Tandon* said.

Santri responded, "Yes, many cadets exhibit this kind of carelessness while performing duties."

Major Yogi replied, "But be alert to the armoury's duty."

Major Tandon reassured everyone confidently. "Don't worry, we are more than 400 cadets here and the armoury is heavily guarded, so the chances of theft are extremely low."

In the night, *Major Tandon* and *Major Romeo* reported to the duty guard on time. The previous duty guards commended their punctuality and handed over the responsibilities to them. They diligently inspected the armoury, ensuring everything was in order before beginning their shift. The guard also briefed them about the responsibilities of their shift. They both listened attentively and looked eager to fulfill their duties diligently, but despite their pretence, they slept near the temple after some formalities, as planned. The night was quiet and peaceful, with only the occasional sound of crickets breaking the silence. Both found solace in the stillness as they settled down on the mattress, ready to catch up on some much-needed rest.

Unexpectedly, *Major Tandon* was immersed in the dream world, his mind drifting away from the responsibilities and tasks that awaited him in the morning. As he slept, his face relaxed and became peaceful, a stark contrast to the focused and determined expression he wore during the day. The serenity of the night provided him with much-needed relaxation from the pressures of his role, and he imagined Alexander's army base and soldiers moving here and there at midnight.

Alexender's Army base:

The commotion was deafening, and some soldiers caught a young boy while others were yelling, 'Kill the unfaithful' 'Hang this devious man' 'This will not be part of Alexander's army'. Suddenly, an officer more mature than young soldiers appeared and caught that young boy with his hands. His robust physique and vigorous shoulders, as well as the sword around the waist, indicate that he was a proficient commander. The commander was looking respectful in the army because of his reach;

he reached directly into Alexander's ample private space in the war zone.

When he arrived, the other soldiers saluted him, and he walked straight into Alexander's ample space. In the dim light of the fire, only the commander's face with a cut mark and the young boy were noticeable.

The area around Alexander's tent had intense lighting, and there were powerful weapons all around it. The commander's confident demeanour and the soldiers' immediate salute further solidified his reputation as a seasoned leader. The commander easily passed through the three layers of security and met with Alexander. As he entered Alexander's tent, the young boy's eyes widened with awe, realizing the immense power and authority the commander holds, but in the shadow of a bright light, Alexander appeared hazy.

The troop commander saluted Alexander and stated, "Sir, the situation is getting worse by the day. My unit recently apprehended a traitor and wants to punish them; they want to kill the traitor, and soldiers are growing impatient. In my opinion, impatience is detrimental in war; a soldier should be calm and disciplined. Take the appropriate action, sir. Troops are losing faith and altering their behaviour in the current situation. Sir, the growing impatience among the soldiers not only poses a threat to discipline but also undermines morale and unity within the army. It is crucial to address this issue promptly to prevent further deterioration of the situation. Additionally, a swift and fair resolution regarding the punishment of the traitor will help restore faith in leadership and ensure that our troops remain focused on their mission. Recently, I informed them that Alexander would decide on this traitor, but they would wait for your decision."

Alexander armed himself and tightened his belts. He also noticed that royal guards had apprehended a young boy. Curiosity piqued, Alexander inquired about the boy's involvement, demanded an explanation from the guards, and approached the mob.

Alexander skipped the mob and asked the boy, "Do you want to quit this army campaign and be afraid of death?"

The young boy boldly declared, "No, I am not afraid of death."

Alexander approached the boy, looked at him intently, and then said, "There are no marks on your body; it means you have not experienced any war or been involved in any fight till now."

The young boy answered quickly, "Marks appear on those soldiers; enemies eventually strike them, but up till now no enemy has touched me; my agility not only defeated the enemy but also killed them."

"Then why are you leaving the army if you're such a good fighter?" said Alexander.

"I will give you an appropriate gift, and I will promote you to a high position," Alexander said after a brief pause.

"I don't see any compelling reason to fight. I have witnessed the devastating consequences of war. When I look back on the war, all I see are dead bodies, sorrow, and a scream of pain, and I cannot bear the thought of contributing to more suffering." The young boy said,

"And I don't want any big positions or gifts," he added.

The young boy's straightforward thoughts impressed Alexander, and he replied loudly. "Right, a true soldier doesn't fight for these frivolous things."

In between the communication, he also noticed that the boy had a long nose, a strong muscular body, and a royal demeanour. He also realized that the boy was mistreated and not a traitor.

He deceived him and said, "I think, in your family, there is no legacy of sacrifices; that's why you dread losing your life."

"No, this is not the issue; I have no fear of losing my life, and my father and grandfather all have in the Macedonian army," the young boy said confidently.

Alexander: "Okay, it means the shine of anklets and the chimes of bangles are blocking your way. You're stuck in the luxury and enjoyment of life."

"No, that's not the true reason." The young boy yelled loudly.

"So, what is the genuine reason to leave? Tell me specifically," said Alexander.

"No, I'm not sure, but when I was talking to a wounded enemy soldier, he reprimanded me by saying 'External aggressor and you are on my territory, and I am defending my motherland' At that moment, I had no compelling reason to engage in battle with him, but he had a strong motive and reason to war with me."

The young boy paused for a moment and said "It forced me to realize that there is a deeper sense of purpose to war. As a soldier, it's my duty that drives me to fight, but it is something I haven't quite discovered yet. Perhaps it's not about luxury or enjoyment but finding my sense of belonging and purpose in this world."

In the meantime, Troop commander Shaitan Singh interrupts and shouts to the young boy, "Stupid, we are fighting for Alexander and the great dream of a world winner; this dream is not sufficient; the thought of conquering the world does not appeal to you to fight; what else do you need?"

"I am not here to satisfy Alexander's dream; I am here as a soldier of Macedonia. I will fight for the dignity and glory of my homeland. My purposes originate in defending Macedonia's values and ensuring a better future for our people." The young boy announced to crow.

"Yes, I agree; you are not here to fulfil my dreams, but remember, fighting for Motherland is a very prevalent reason to fight; it is justified, and I am an eyewitness to the bravery of weak peoples who use weapons to protect their motherland," Alexander modestly responded.

Alexander took a step forward in front of the increasing crowd and said, "We the soldiers of Macedonia attack the opponent, as a commander I see fear in the eyes of the opposition, but I've never seen fear in a Macedonian soldier. Our determination to fight is unparalleled. We are not fighting for a swath of land or a kingdom but for future generations. This is the unwavering spirit that has allowed us to conquer lands and establish a vast empire, making Macedonia a force to be reckoned with in the world." Alexander's words resonated with the crowd, igniting a newfound sense of pride and unity among his fellow soldiers.

He also added, "I take over vast swaths of land and numerous kingdoms with the help of you, but we're not just fighting for territory or gold; we're fighting to set a high standard of warfare. We intend to set a high bar for bravery. Remember, you are not just soldiers; you are Alexander's soldiers. On the battlefield, we have no greed; we are the ultimate soldiers, and the battle is the ultimate duty of a soldier. Your unwavering loyalty and unmatched courage will inspire countless warriors to follow your path. Together, we will create a great legacy that will be remembered by generations, and we will be remembered as the pioneers of a new era in warfare; our victories will echo through the ages, inspiring generations of warriors."

The crowd chants, "World Winner Alexander, World Winner Alexander!"

Alexander addressed again when the crowd stopped shouting: "My friends, we will build more dangerous weapons. We will plan a more decisive strategy and destroy the enemy. We are opening the religion of war. Believe me, future armies and soldiers will swear in your name."

The crowd chants, "World Winner Alexander, World Winner Alexander."

As a result of Alexender's arguments, the noise increased dramatically, and the young boy also joined the crowd and started to yell. The crowd also raised the flag high in the sky, but suddenly that flag caught fire, and crowd slogans changed, and they were shouting, "Fire, Fire, Fire."

An abrupt noise interrupted *Major Tandon* and Romeo's slumber in the night. *Major Tandon* awoke from his dream, opened his eyes, and saw a massive fire in the temple area. The flames were engulfing the temple, growing larger by every moment, threatening to consume everything in their path. Cadets were throwing water and dust on it. Despite their efforts, the fire continues to rage, spreading rapidly and intensifying. *Major Romeo* was astounded to see that view, and both were at a loss for words. The temple caught fire with its lamp. The flaming fire was too intense, but the weaponry was safe because other cadets were alert. *Major Romeo* and *Major Tandon* were both mute bystanders waiting for the punishment.

Suddenly, the camp senior approached and inquired, 'Who was performing the duty here?' and *Major Tandon* quickly raised his hand proudly. The camp senior was looking at *Major Tandon* with a mix of surprise and damnation.

Story 11

Girls in The Camp

The story of the 'boy's' first encounter with 'girls' in the camp

The Army has been a primarily male-dominated organization since ancient times, irrespective of regions throughout the globe. It is a widely accepted fact that the battlefield is only made for males, and the meaning of masculinity is either strength or fight. Similarly, we had been familiar with the word 'boys' in our training because we knew that only boys were available in our troop; conversely, this camp was unique when we first encountered the girl wing. The girls not only pervaded the camp's discipline but also created a helpful atmosphere in a typically monotonous environment. Their presence brought a new perspective and energy to the camp.

The moment in a camp where *Major Tandon* was digging the snake trench outside the tent while cleaning the sweat and told *Major Romeo*, "Hey major, it is mandatory to dig the entire trench line by today itself."

Major Romeo: "Yes, because *Subedar Saab* will inspect all tents tomorrow and give the markings."

Major Tandon: "Marking? What kind of marking?"

"Yes, there are about ten competitions in this camp, and after each competition, our battalion will get the marks out of 100. The battalion that gets the highest mark will win the trophy," *Major Romeo* said.

"Yes, I know," *Major Tandon* said, "but what's the connection between these competitions and the trench line?"

"Tent decoration and management are also part of the competition, and the trench line has a high mark weightage" *Major Romeo* replied.

Major Tandon: "Is this competition not starting so early?"

"Because you're enjoying the entire day without PT and the parade, that's why camp officials are focusing on trench lines," *Major Yogi* explained.

Major Tandon: I was also surprised to hear that there is no PT or parade in this camp.

Major Yogi: Despite that, you are enjoying dance, music, and eating ice cream every evening.

Santri: "Yeah, ice cream was delicious; I ate it for the first time in the camp."

"All right, then come here and dig the trench line and give something back to the camp," *Major Romeo* said, raising his spade towards the *Santri.*

Suddenly, *Santri* remembered something and told the other cadets, "Boys, good news, it's teatime; you can take a nap, and I am arranging water and bringing tea for you from the mess." He moved towards the canteen, carrying a bucket with '2 *MP Arty Bty*' written on it.

"I'll complain to ANO because he never works as a team," *Major Tandon* said, showing his anger towards *Santri.*

Major Yogi: "Don't be angry; his weak hands can't handle the weight of a spade. Tea and water arrangements suit him."

Santri eventually appeared with water and tea, and they all drank tea in the shadow of the tent and finished digging a trench. Our unit finished the tent decoration by the evening and made some extra arrangements, such as placing sand and a water bucket outside the tent in case of fire, installing a mirror for an impressive turnoff, and setting up the tent's interiors. We all put a lot of effort into decorating the tent until dusk.

Since all the work had been completed. Our SUO was feeling relaxed for the upcoming inspection at night. On the other hand, we were relaxing inside the tent. We had exhausted and injured to make these arrangements.

Major Romeo told *Major AG*, "Hey, Major, if the inspection does not happen tomorrow, we will all punish you."

Major AG: "Believe me, *Subedar Saab* conveyed that message and assured me that we are going to receive the highest marks in this category."

The discussion came to an end, and everyone sat down for the night. The day in camp usually started early in the camp, and the mornings were chilled. The cold wind and smog were creating a chilly environment, but cadets were preparing themselves for the inspection. Suddenly, *Subedar Saab* announced an unexpected roll call in the morning and directed all cadets and officers to assemble on the ground immediately. While waiting in the queue of N-threes of roll call, we were thinking about something ominous. Suddenly, we noticed that girls of the Air Wing in blue uniforms were advancing to the parade ground in a disciplined manner. Our gaze was drawn to a tall, attractive, and fair-skinned young girl, SUO of the air wing. On the other side, we saw our SUO, who is a tiny black boy who is standing in front of the girl's wing.

Major Tandon unexpectedly raised his voice, saying, "It's the right time to replace the SUO."

Major AG: Why?

Major Tandon: After all, it's about the 2 MP Artillery Battalion's reputation because our officer looks like a monkey.

Major Yogi said, "Not just like a monkey, but like a black monkey."

Major Romeo added, "Yes, girls will think that artillery doesn't have any other handsome officers."

Major AG replies, Friends, please keep your mouth shut; I am unable to listen to the instructions.

Abruptly, *Subedar Saab* said, "Listen, boys, the 09 MP Air Wing has already joined us, and one more

Girls Wing will join us soon, till the evening, and I am providing the space to them on the left side."

Major Tandon: Is *Subedar Saab* showing our tent area?

Yes, *Major Romeo* replied.

"I am giving you the time till the afternoon to set up the new tent, and don't try to become smart because I know how to reflow the blood to your head." *Subedar Saab* said, pointing toward the two students who were getting punishment for becoming '*Tanks*'.

As the roll call finished, *Major Yogi* replied, "This isn't a fair competition; it's cheating."

Major Tandon pointed toward the *Major AG* and said, "I don't trust this person; he can't do anything right."

Inside the tent, *Santri* excitedly asked the troop, "So the competition is over."

Major Tandon: No, our tent has been given to the girls.

Santri surprisingly asked, "Are there girls in the camp? I'm glad to know that."

"Don't be happy," said *Major Romeo*. "They are stronger than you."

Santri: I will not leave that tent, and we can inform *Subedar Saab* that we have already dug the trench line and properly decorated it, so we will not leave. We have no problems if the girls have settled into the other nearby tents.

Major Yogi: I know you won't have any problems, but girls may have problems with you. They will complain about seeing a chimpanzee near the tent area.

Major Romeo: Let's stop fighting and think about what we can do in this difficult situation.

Major AG: We have no other option but to leave this tent.

Major Tandon: But we can destroy all the decoration and fill the trench line, which is no longer usable, the same as the scorched earth policy.

"No, we're not going to do anything ridiculous like a *'Scorched Earth Policy'*, and for your kind information, *'Scorched Earth Policy'* is banned under the Geneva Convention," *Major Romeo* replied.

"But others are retaliating and destroying all the arrangements," *Major Tandon* said.

Major Romeo: No, I don't care what the others are doing, but as artillery soldiers, we will do a significant job.

Major AG: I think Romeo is right.

Major Tandon: "So you're not in a fighting mood; you're giving these girls a walkover."

Major Romeo: What fights? We're not at war.

Major Tandon: But we are competitors; we are here to win a trophy for our battalion.

Santri: "Ignore the competition now; it's over and enjoy the presence of girls."

Major Tandon: "No, it's not over; it's just started."

Major Romeo: "But we are not going to destroy anything in this tent."

Major Tandon: So, you can put some flowers inside the tent as well.

Major Romeo: "Yes, it's a good idea; we can do this."

Major AG: That is an excellent suggestion, and luckily this is the sacred month of February.

Major Romeo: Yes, I have already identified the colourful flowers available near the tent area.

Major Tandon: All right, you do this bewildering thing; I will pack and move. But don't forget the tank.

Santri: Tank? What is this tank?

Major Tandon: It is a form of punishment in which you simultaneously put your legs and head on the ground, and blood starts flowing toward your head. Within a minute, your mind will be cleansed of all negativities, and in the next five minutes, you will be unable to maintain your balance on the ground.

Major Yogi told *Tandon*: Don't get upset, we are soldiers, we are different from others. Be mature, and trust me, it will benefit us.

After some coaxing, *Major Tandon* finally agreed to leave the tent as it is, with flowers, and *Santri* separated himself from all this activity.

Two days later,

The troop was discussing something inside the tent in the dim light of a bulb after dinner.

Major Tandon said solemnly, "It's a grave matter; we're fifth in the parade."

Major Yogi: We're lagging behind the girl wing.

Major Romeo: No, we're boys, and the girls have defeated us.

Major Yogi: Yes, I was thinking they wouldn't be able to handle the guns, but they are experts with the weaponry.

Major Romeo: We are already in fifth place in the tent decoration competition.

Major Tandon: That's why I was telling you to destroy all the arrangements in the tent, but you placed flowers in the tent.

Major AG: Please forget about the past and concentrate on the future.

Major Tandon: Future? What future? We are not going to secure third place in the overall competition.

Major AG: Yes, Major, you are correct because there are only a few competitions left. We can hope for music because we have a flute player; otherwise, girls can easily oust us in singing and dancing.

Major Romeo: Don't give up! We can do better and will win over the girls.

Santri: Don't try to fool us; I saw both of you talking to the girl.

"I am not remembering," *Major AG* exclaimed angrily.

Santri: "That tall, lovely girl, the commander of the girl wing."

Major Romeo: "No, I am not remembering."

Santri: "Remember that day when you were discussing with the girl and saying that your undisciplined curly hairs are not following your orders and behaving like rebels?"

Major Romeo smiled and said: "Oh, yes, yes, I remember."

Major AG: We were attempting to steal information from the opponent.

Santri: So, what information have you gathered?

Major Romeo replied quietly: "A lot".

Major AG: Many more.

Major Tandon asked angrily, "Will you please explain in detail?"

Major Romeo: Okay, now pay close attention and listen carefully; these are not typical adolescent girls. They are well-prepared and unbeatable, and they will be in Delhi next month for the Republic Day parade. They have also received extensive training from the army, and some of them are musicians, dancers, and singers. But the interesting thing is that they are willing to assist us in the music and dancing competition to secure a respectable position in this competition.

Santri: Swear to me that you're not lying.

Major Romeo: "Believe me, it's only because of those flowers."

"It was my idea," *Major Tandon* said.

"Of course, I remembered that day when you were suggesting some better ideas to us," *Major Romeo* said immediately.

Major Tandon pretended to sleep after this conversation by turning his head to the other side.

Major Romeo said with an authoritative voice: "All right, cadets, be ready for the next-day event where *SUO KS2234* will come and help us in dancing competitions, and this will not only furnish our performance but also help us to achieve a respectable position in the competition.

Santri: But what about *Colonel Saab*?

Major Romeo: Don't worry; he will also appreciate it. You can recall yesterday's speech when he mentioned that 'the trophy is only for the best company, but never forget that we are the soldiers first, and it is our duty as soldiers to help one another.'

On the morning of the dance competition,

Major Tandon questioned Romeo, "How can we change our dance performance a few hours before the competition?"

Major Romeo: Don't worry, we are not going to change our performance; we are just replacing the girl.

Major Tandon: where will we find a girl at this last moment?

Major AG: Don't worry, *SUO KS2234* is ready to provide the country dress.

Major Tandon: What will we do with the dress? How can we arrange a girl at that last moment?

Santri: But why does *Cadet SS3342* refuse to dance with us?

Major Romeo: *SUO KS2234* and *Cadet SS3342* both abide by the rule.

Santri: What kind of rule?

Major Romeo: None of the cadets from other battalions can take part in the competition.

Santri: So, what is the problem with this rule? how people will judge her, she is not from our battalion.

Major Romeo: Because our battalion has no girl wing, how can a girl perform with us?

Santri: So why did she suggest a dance in which we dance with country-dressed women?

Major Romeo: Because she was trying for our victory and wanted to improve our performance.

Major Tandon: So, what will we do now?

Major AG: No idea.

Santri: So, we are not going to dance today, and a negative marking disqualifies us from the competition.

Major Romeo: The problem will be solved if a cadet of our battalion agrees to wear a girl's country dress and dance with us.

Major Tandon: Are you mad? Is it possible for a boy to dress like a woman?

Major Romeo: But this is the only way we can secure a respectable position.

Major Yogi: Okay, I will find a suitable boy for this job.

Major Romeo: That's wonderful, and I'll arrange the country attire.

One hour later, *Romeo* came back with all the jewellery and folk costumes, but both *Major Yogi* and *Major Tandon* had seated with dull looks on their faces.

Major Romeo: Have you found a boy who performs the girl's dance?

Major Yogi: No.

Major Romeo: Why?

"They are all the sons of great *Maharana Pratap*, born for fighting and feeling insulted to wear a girl's costume," *Major Yogi* said, pointing to the group of cadets.

Major Romeo: "Oh, it's a serious issue. Did you cite the *Great Pandavas Arjun* as an example?"

Major Yogi: Twice, but they refused the idea every time.

Major AG: So, ultimately, we are not going to dance performance.

"Don't worry, we'll perform the dance and take home the trophy," *Major Romeo* replied.

Major Tandon: How.

Major Romeo: "I have a plan"

Major Yogi said casually, please tell.

Major Romeo: Any one of us can become a girl.

Major Tandon: No, it is not possible.

Major Yogi: Don't look at me.

Major AG: How does a black boy turn into a girl? How will I look with this black beard and mustache?

"It's not a big problem; you can shave," *Major Romeo* said.

"Why not you?" asked *Major AG*.

"So, no one is concerned about our battalion's reputation," *Major Romeo* declared.

They all flat-out replied, No,

No,

No,

Ok, we can use play cards to choose the person. I will distribute the cards to all of us and who will get the queen first he will become the girl, *Major Romeo* replied.

"Yes, I agree," said *Major Yogi*.

Major Tandon: Sure.

Major AG: Yes, I agree.

Major Romeo: "But remember, once this game started, no one can quit.

Major Yogi: I agree.

Major Tandon: I agree.

Major AG: "However, there is one condition from my end." He paused for a minute and said, "Nobody will disclose the chosen person's identity."

Major Romeo said happily, "Yes, we all agree."

The tent echoed with relief and disappointment. The competition concluded late in the night, and everyone appreciated our efforts. Of course, we did well, and our battalion got a respectable position in the competition. *Colonel Saab* also appreciated the performance of the girl, even though he didn't know she was not a girl. Some of the battalion's officers and soldiers voiced their disapproval of the performance, questioning how a boy could play the girl's role. On the night of the campfire party, everyone was asking us, 'Who was the girl last night?' and, in accordance with the covenant, the mystery had been concealed.

Story 12

The Fairies of Kerala

The story includes a delightful moment of tracking camp

The troop of junior cadets was returning to the mess hall, joyfully discussing that today's dinner was delicious, particularly the butter chicken.

A cadet asked *Santri*, "But why don't we get butter chicken every day?

Santri answered, "In the Kerala tracking camp, we got butter chicken every day. Are you interested in knowing more about the delights of the Kerala tracking camp?"

'Yes, sir'; they all said it unanimously.

Santri halted the group near a tree, and all the cadets seated near the lounge. *Santri* secured a superior place in the lounge beneath the tree, where he could watch every cadet of the troop. When all the cadets settled down, *Santri* started the story of Kerela Camp.

It was a gleaming night, and the moon was sparkling in the sky. We were all gathered at the railway station, excitedly waiting for the train that would take us to the magical land of Kerala. We had no idea what kind of adventures were waiting for us in that magical land. The journey started late at night, but the real wonder emerged in the morning when *Romeo* woke me up early to look outside. When I looked outside, I saw a beautiful green mountain with a white milky cloud covering the peak, and our train was approaching it. The morning was chilly, yet we all remained at the window to admire the vista. After an hour, our train stopped at a deserted station, which I believe was a magnificent hill station. We had never seen a hill station or mountain before, so this was a new and exciting experience for all of us. The air was fresh and crisp, and the silence of the surroundings made it feel like we were in a different world altogether. The slope and station amazed and gladdened us within.

We had travelled approximately fifty hours, and our train strolled through mountains, rivers, and forests to reach Kerala. Kerala was a lovely place where we saw beautiful houses, canals, and a rich culture. The lush greenery and vibrant wildlife added to the charm of the place, creating a picturesque landscape that was a feast for the eyes. The sight was truly breathtaking and set the tone for the rest of the camp experience.

We approached the campsite early in the morning, but it was not the usual campsite; instead, it seemed to be a movie set. We were amazed to see a dam with a canal with a constant flow of water, tourist quarters, a large mountain range, and tall trees. We stayed in a lovely tourist quarter, which was obviously in poor condition but much superior to the tent. On the backside of the quarter, there was a window from which we could see the dam's backwater and all five peaks in the huge mountain range. It was a heaven on earth, and we were all awestruck by its beauty.

There was also a lion safari on the island of Dam's backwaters, where visitors could get a close-up view of majestic lions in their natural habitat. Crocodiles and alligators were found in the surrounding water, adding to the thrill of our camp experience. The diverse wildlife and stunning scenery made our stay in the tourist quarter even more memorable.

However, there was one problem with the drinking water: all the cadets were advised to drink boiled water that was hot and reddish-coloured due to some medicine or treatment. Despite the hot and unpleasant taste of the water, it was a small price to pay for the amazing opportunity to encounter the constant roar of lions throughout the day and see crocodiles and alligators in their natural habitat.

The next morning, as usual, as we were getting ready for PT in our barracks, we noticed that it had heavily rained the night before, filling the dam and keeping the canal flowing constantly with huge noise. Our PT had cancelled, but we met our PT instructor, who taught us two important things during the warm-up: the motto of his unit, *'Jai Maa Kali, Aaya Gorakhali.'*

Suddenly, *Cadet Rambo* asked the *Santri*, "What's the second, sir?"

Santri: Another two things.

Alex: What are they?

Santri: *Boot* and *Rangroot* (Shoes and soldiers)

Cadet Rambo: Are both the same?

Santri: No, *Boot* and *Rangroot*, both; the more you rub, the more it shines.

The cadets were all enraged as they remembered their toil, but *Santri* remained calm and continued his conversation. He said, In the warm-up, I observed a very mysterious thing in the camp area. A group of foreigners were walking down the street, singing a holy song, while beautiful girls cheered them on. Our PT instructor was paying close attention to that drama. We were also curious about the group of foreigners, but they were heading to the forbidden back side of the campsite. We set two goals on that day, first, to reach the topmost peak of the campsite, which had piqued our interest, and second, to explore the mysterious forbidden land of foreigners.

Our schedule was set in the camp, and every day in the morning we explored the whole campsite through small marathons with our PT trainer. In the afternoon, we practiced mountain tracking and river crossing near the canal after breakfast. The day ended with a cultural evening where cadets danced and sang to demonstrate their talents and ate delicious butter chicken every day.

"O gallan goriyan de vich toye

Assi mar gaye ni oye hoye

O gallan goriyan de vich toye

Assi mar gaye ni oye hoye

Oye hoye duhayi peh gayi,

O kudi katke kaalja le gayi

O gallan goriyan de vich toye"

He was lost in memory for some time and said, Boys, Punjabi cadets sang that incredible song in the camp, and we cheerfully played the *Thali* and *Katori* to accompany them. The cadets from throughout the country were there, Delhi, Punjab, Kashmir, Maharashtra, and Odisha, and represented the rich culture of great India. Those days were filled with so much magic.

Suddenly, a cadet asked him about the mysterious, forbidden land.

Santri replied, "After five days of camp, we were still unaware of the mysterious, forbidden land. The main issue was language because most of the cadets spoke their native tongues. Finally, we found a cadet who could communicate in English using some Malayalam words, and we deduced something about the forbidden place. It was the hermitage of a saint, and the foreigners were the saint's followers. Boys, we knew that if we wanted to explore the hermitage, it would require perfect planning and coordination.

Santri stretched his legs, broadened on the platform, and said, "With each passing day, our excitement grew as we anticipated the challenges. The camp was running on time, and we had finished our river crossing training and were getting ready for the next."

Cadet Rambo asked, "How did you cross the river?"

Santri responded, "Oh, I forgot to mention the river crossing training; it was truly a brave event, and only a few brave soldiers were selected for the final competition, and I was one of them. In the training, we learned how to tie a knot and then first-man and second-man knots if you are tracking in the group. We were excited and waiting for the final challenge when our trainer determined that we had received adequate training. The rope bridge had already been constructed, where the final competition would be performed."

Santri's eyes gleamed with light when he spoke about the final test. He exuded confidence and said, In the final test, I was hanged on the rope like a monkey, and my entire body mass was resting on an iron bolt. My gaze was fixed on the sky, and I noticed a river with massive waves on the downside. The final test was designed to challenge your physical strength and mental fortitude. It required your trust in whatever you learned, knot-tying skills, and the ability to overcome any fear of heights. But I bravely hung there, crossed the river, and reached the other end of the rope successfully.

Cadet Alex inquired, "Really, sir, you crossed the entire river without incident?"

"I'm not lying at all, and if you have any doubts, Romeo's camera caught everything," *Santri* responded quickly.

"You captured the movement on the camera; you have a camera inside the camp?" *Cadet Alex* exclaimed in awe.

Santri now turned into full relaxation mode, stretched his whole body like a king, and said, "Do you think that I can't do any courageous work?"

"No, sir, we believe in you," *Cadet Rambo* replied.

Santri replied, "Yes, belief is a wonderful feeling, but you will be amazed when you see the photographs."

"Sir, in photographs, you will be looking handsome," *Cadet Rambo* questioned.

Santri replied, "Yes, I always look handsome in uniform, but I think my lovely picture was captured on the top of the hill."

Cadet Alex asked, "Really, sir, did you get to the top of the hill and capture pictures there?"

"The story of how we reached the top of the hill was also very interesting," *Santri* replied with gleaming eyes once again. He continued, "After crossing the river, our next target was to climb to the top of the hill. Our path up the hill wound through steep slopes and dense forest. On the contrary, heavy rain could pour down the hill at any time, complicating our journey. We had to be cautious and keep an eye on the weather conditions to ensure our safety. Of course, it was quite a challenging task, but the view from the top made it all worth it.

We were ready to climb toward the hill on the assumed date. Our commanding officer separated us into three major groups. Each group was assigned a specific task and instructed to work together to ensure the success of the mission. We were all prepared with all the equipment and supplies necessary for the climb. Our backpacks were filled with ropes and other essentials. Additionally, we had packed enough food and water to supply us throughout the journey. With our equipment in place, we were feeling confident and ready to face any challenges that awaited us on the way. We were determined to complete our tasks and make our commanding officer proud. We had trained extensively for this mission, and each member of the team was committed to giving their best effort and supporting one another. However, we were running behind schedule due to unforeseen circumstances. Despite this setback, we remained focused and determined to reach our destination safely. We adjusted our pace and strategized to return to the campsite before dark.

Abruptly, *Cadet Rambo* inquired, "So, you reached the top of the hill?"

"No, we took the wrong path and appeared on the other side of the hill by mistake," *Santri* replied straightforwardly.

Cadet Alex curiously inquired, "Then what happened?"

Santri explained, "But on the other side of the hill, we saw gorgeous springs and beautiful pineapple farms that extended for miles. It was a pleasant surprise and a silver lining to our unexpected detour. We took a moment to appreciate the stunning scenery before finding our way back on track and continuing our journey. We enjoyed ourselves there and took pictures of the hill and spring. We accidentally discovered the true beauty of the mountain and have had a great time with nature. It turned out to be a pleasant surprise amidst our unexpected detours."

Cadet Rambo asked, "So you did not reach the top of the hill in the end?"

"No, because we're on the other side of the hill, we can't see the dark cloud coming from the south, and we also don't know what the other two teams have decided, and we keep climbing to the top without thinking there is any danger. Only our team raised the flag at the top of the hill. Of course, we got trapped in the heavy rain while returning, but we completed our mission successfully," *Santri* said.

Cadet Rambo questioned, "Sir, what about the camera?"

"Till that point, the camera and all the images were safe," *Santri* explained.

"Sir, any damage to the camera after that event?" *Cadet Alex* inquired.

"Not at the top of the hill, but at that mysterious land," *Santri* replied.

"What happened in that mysterious land?" *Cadet Alex* inquired.

"Do you seriously want to hear the story of the fairies of that magical land?" *Santri* inquired.

'Yes, sir' they all said unanimously.

Santri took a deep breath and began recounting the enchanting tale of the fairies and their magical land. As he spoke back, his words painted a vivid picture in his mind, holding them in a world filled with wonder and awe.

Santri said, "We knew it was a hermitage, but how to get there was a mystery. The sturdy barricades were the most difficult obstacle in our path, but we had one advantage. Our tourist quarter was the last quarter of the campsite, and the barricade was only a few meters away from us. We decided to cross the barricade in the morning because some cadets left their duties earlier than usual, and we would take advantage of this opportunity. As the sun was approaching towards latitude, casting a golden glow over the campsite, we silently made our way toward the barricade. We effortlessly passed through the first and then the second barricades. We observed that the sun was watching us hide behind the long trees. Yet I sensed God was present with us that day, and we faced no trouble reaching that magnificent area. After traveling half a kilometre, we noticed a signboard that said, 'Route to Lion Safari,' as well as the threat of wild animals. We were all looking forward fearfully, admiring the beauty of a vast backwater. Suddenly, I noticed the small entrance at the back of that hermitage. Curiosity piqued, and we cautiously approached the entrance, wondering what secrets it held within. We were stunned when we came across some foreign girls taking a dip into the river just outside the hermitage's back entrance. The sight of the foreign girls surprised us, as we hadn't expected to encounter anyone in such a secluded area. They seemed to be enjoying the serene surroundings, unaware of our presence. We hesitated for a moment, unsure whether to continue or find an alternative route to avoid disturbing them.

After a brief pause, *Santri* replied, "All the girls were looking like fairies dancing amidst the untouched beauty of nature. Their laughter made the atmosphere colourful and lively. We were quietly watching them from a distance, in awe of their carefree attitude, because we didn't want to ruin the magical moment. We decided to quietly pass by and didn't want to disturb their peaceful moment. With newfound confidence, we took a collective step forward, venturing into the mysterious land of the fairies, eager to explore and immerse ourselves in its magical beauty."

Cadet Rambo inquired, "Did you cross the road and see the girls playing in the water?"

"Of course, they didn't mind our presence, but that camera created a big blunder there," *Santri* replied.

Cadet Alex asked, "Which kind of blunder, sir?"

In a quiet voice, *Santri* continued, "There is a security check next to the gate, and the security guard suspected that we were capturing images of the girls. He warned us that photography was strictly prohibited in the area to protect the fairies' privacy."

Cadet Alex questioned, "You were taking the pictures, right?"

Santri calmly said, "No, we weren't shooting any photographs, but the nasty security guard removed all the reels from the camera. He even threatened to report our presence to the authorities if we didn't leave immediately. It was quite an unpleasant experience."

"But sir, I've seen the photograph of Kerala's tour posted on the NCC board at the college," *Cadet Rambo* said.

Santri: "Well, some reels had been damaged and are not available now. The photographs that were showcasing my bravery were all ruined."

Santri stood up, dusted his clothes, walked away with a disappointed expression on his face, and instructed all the cadets to go inside the tent. The night had grown too dark, and only the lamp near the office had been switched off. *Santri* was going to bed because he had no duty due to his illness. Two cadets were wearing uniforms and preparing themselves inside the tent for night duty. They were both ready to leave the tent and check their beret cap that was sufficiently entangled. They both discussed with each other.

"I don't believe in *Santri*'s tales," one of them whispered.

"He always exaggerates his accomplishments," the other cadet replied, shaking his head.

"I've heard similar stories from him before, and it always seems too far-fetched to be true." He added.

"Me, too, but I enjoy his storytelling." They both disappeared into the silence of the camp in the night.

Story 13

Yes Sir

The story of fear and dread

We made frequent trips to the battalion office to observe the soldiers' lives. Our battalion office was in the middle of the city, where three big artillery canons (commonly known as 25-Pounders) were situated. We felt proud to touch the masculine body and strong mechanism of the artillery guns. One day at the battalion office, we met with *Major RK*, who was our new training officer in the battalion. His impressive uniform and shining stars attracted us. We started our discussion with *Major RK* by showing our curiosity to know more about the big cannons. He was an expert in the field of artillery, and he explained everything to us about the cannons in detail.

The cannons were amazing, strong, and accurate enough to destroy the enemy tank from more than 10 Kilometers away. *Major RK* emphasized the importance of proper training and maintenance to ensure the cannons' optimal performance on the battlefield. He also shared stories of successful missions where the cannons played a crucial role in turning the tide of battle, leaving us in awe of their capabilities. He quickly judged our curiosity and ordered us to come on Sunday to give proper respect to this gun and make it shine. He also mentioned that the cannons are equipped with advanced targeting systems, allowing them to track and engage multiple targets simultaneously. He encouraged us to witness the power of the cannons firsthand and understand the importance of their role in modern warfare. We all agreed to come on Sunday, gave our confirmation to him, and moved towards our house. While we were riding the bicycle, I asked *Major Yogi*, "Hey Major, I noticed that the *RK's* rank was hidden with a black cover."

Major Yogi: Yes, I have also noticed the same, but why is it so?

Cadet Alex: "I think he doesn't want to show his rank to the public."

Major Yogi: Yes, dear Alex, maybe he is an undercover officer of the army."

Romeo said angrily, Alex, I have two suggestions for you."

Cadet Alex: What they are?

Major Romeo: "First and foremost, for God's sake, please stop thinking."

During this discussion, *Major Yogi* chuckled and said, "You don't want to hear another suggestion."

"No, I have some work, so please inform Mummy that I will be late," *Cadet Alex* told *Major Romeo*.

Major Yogi: "Don't be upset, *Yaar*. Please be with us until the second suggestion."

"What is the second suggestion?" *Major Yogi* asked *Major Romeo* to grab the handle of Alex's bicycle.

"If, by mistake, you have an idea, please don't share it with the public; maintain the secrecy of that precious thought," *Major Romeo* said angrily.

After the second suggestion, *Cadet Alex* wasn't ready to go with us, and *Major Yogi*'s request didn't change his mind. We finally reached our home in various ways and patiently waited for Sunday. We dressed in proper uniform on Sunday and were ready to go to the battalion office. We had started training early in the morning and spent the day washing and polishing the canons.

Major RK asked us, "Would you like to target practice with this gun?"

We all agreed and enthusiastically said, "Yes, sir."

Initially, he gave a briefing on the aiming system of the gun, and then we started the practice. He demonstrated the proper techniques for loading and aiming the cannon, emphasizing the importance of precision and accuracy. He shared stories of the cannon's earlier days of pelting the enemy with gunpowder and flames, highlighting its destructive power on the battlefield. As we listened attentively, our excitement grew, eager to experience the thrill of firing such a historic weapon.

He shouted in his powerful voice, "Boys, it needs four soldiers and an officer to operate this cannon. For target practice, we'll divide into two teams: the Friends Team and the Enemy Team. Both teams will examine the gun's stability, identify the enemy's coordinates, altitude, and azimuth, and then lock the target. Do you understand the task?

'Yes, sir,' we all responded unanimously.

The training exercise started by placing the cannons on the ground. The cannons could aim in 360 degrees or every possible direction. The gun was already equipped with a binocular and a prism for measuring altitude and azimuth, but we used an army binocular, which was far superior to a regular binocular. As science students, we acquainted to the gun quickly and became familiar with the technical terms of artillery training. We understood all the instructions quickly in comparison to other students until the afternoon. Our team practiced and switched their roles from friend to foe. During my free time in the afternoon, I asked *Sargeant MS* the other training officer of our battalion, 'Why does *Major RK* keep his rank secret?'. He smiled first and suggested to us, 'Why don't you ask *Billa*?'

Billa was also a training officer in our artillery battalion, but he was famous for his strict disciplinary approach. His full name was *Major*

KS, but his friends referred to him as *Billa*. We never tried to find what this *Billa* meant, but *Major Tandon* surmised that "he is short-statured, shrewd, round-faced, and his mustaches are very thin, like a cat; that's why *Billa* resembles him."

The training was approaching an end for the day, but the question remained unanswered, prompting a new critical question: 'Who would approach *Billa* and inquire?' *Major Romeo* questioned everyone, 'Who will come with me?' but everyone had different reasons to deny it.

Major Tandon: I will not go up to him. He is very nasty.

Romeo inquired again, "Have you ever received a punishment from *Billa*?"

Major Tandon answered quietly, "Yes, *Alex* and I were coming back from the officer mess in the last camp; of course, that was a forbidden area of the camp, but *Billa* pounced on both of us."

Major Romeo: Did he punish you? What exactly happened there?

Major Tandon: No, he simply ordered us to turn back and march forward until further order.

Major Romeo: Then what happened? Did you march?

Major Tandon: Yes, we were marching and waiting for further orders for 10 minutes, up to 300 meters.

Major Romeo: Did you turn around and look back?

Major Tandon: No, he had already warned us that if we looked back, he would punish us. We were both terrified by his commanding voice.

Major Romeo: When you get the order to stop.

Major Tandon: No, no orders came in. Another officer spotted us marching at night and shouted at us, saying, why are you marching at 11 o'clock? And when we turned back, we noticed that *Billa* wasn't there.

Major Romeo: That's incredible. But what did that officer tell you? How did you convince them?

Major Tandon: We told him we were both practicing drills for an upcoming competition, and he appreciated our sincere efforts as well.

Major Yogi: Don't worry; we've already encountered *Billa*. Do you want to know what happened to us?

'Yes,' *Major Tandon* replied timidly.

Major Yogi: One day in camp, during the parade session, *Billa* was punishing our entire section and ordered us to run to the mess and bring the leaf of the Banyan tree; I will consider only the first five cadets. As he ordered us, we all ran quickly, but in the middle of the road, *Romeo* told me, 'We can take any banyan tree leaf and be the first to reach there' We quickly grabbed a banyan tree leaf from a nearby tree and beat everyone else.

Major Tandon: That's correct; *Romeo* is always able to find a simple solution in difficult situations. But what happened next?

Major Yogi: There was no banyan tree in the vicinity of the mess.

Major Tandon: What happened after that?

Major Yogi: That is not important, but I won't go to *Billa* to talk about this critical matter.

Major Romeo: So that's your final decision; you're not coming with me.

Major Tandon: Yes, we are not going with you, and as a good friend, I will suggest you don't go there.

Major Romeo: Don't offer any suggestions to me; I've made up my mind. I think you have forgotten the motto of the NCC.

Major Tandon: 'Unity and Discipline'

Major Romeo: Yes, recall the 'Unity'.

Major Yogi: Yes, of course, but please also mention discipline.

Major Tandon: But as a good friend, I will suggest, 'Please drop that idea and go home with us'.

Major Romeo: I think you are missing what we've learned in the NCC.

Major Romeo roared in a firm voice, '*Ladenge*' and both (*Major Yogi* and *Major Tandon*) accompanied them unanimously by saying, '*Akhiri Saans Tak*'. After this announcement, *Major Tandon* said, Romeo, what can we say if you blackmail us using this motivational slogan; Finally *Major Tandon* and *Major Yogi* agreed to go with *Major Romeo*. They all approached *Billa* and saluted him. *Billa* smiled first, and his thin mustache rose to his cheek as usual.

Major Tandon inquired *Billa*, "Sir, you are not taking part in the cleaning drill?"

Billa: Do you want to learn with me?

Major Yogi: Of course, sir, you are also an expert in gunnery and artillery.

Billa smiled again and added, "When I was stationed in Kashmir, my unit was credited with a significant event."

Major Tandon: What's that event, sir? Please share.

Billa: We destroyed an enemy post, and when we recaptured it, our light infantry soldiers informed us that we had destroyed the enemy's cannon by inserting the cannonball into its mouth.

Major Tandon: Wow, it's incredible, sir.

Major Yogi: But we are aware of it, sir.

Billa: How?

Major Tandon: *Colonel Saab* has already shared the events with us.

Billa: Yes, I was on the same team.

Major Romeo: Sir, I believe you were getting revenge for something during that mission.

Billa: No, there is no room for emotion in military operations.

Major Romeo: So, what motivates you to do this risky activity?

Major Tandon: No doubt, soldiers fight for their motherland.

Major Yogi: Yes, patriotism. I believe patriotism motivates soldiers to fight.

Billa rejected all the options and proclaimed, "Patriotism, *huh*? When bombardment comes in all possible ways, your *'Patriotism'* on the battlefield disappears."

Major Romeo: So, what motivates you to assassinate the enemy on the battlefield?

Billa: Do you want to know?

Major Romeo: Yes, sir, we want to know what is more important than patriotism for a soldier like you.

Billa abruptly stood up and declared, "Discipline; discipline prepares and inspires us to perform courageous tasks. But no matter how brilliant or brave you are, you will harm the unit and your fellow soldiers if you don't have discipline."

"Why is a black ribbon covering *Major RK's* rank on his shoulder?" *Romeo* asked *Billa*.

Billa looked at us straight on for a moment and then said, "As a soldier, you must obey orders; always say 'Yes sir' without any question."

He added, "You understand what I'm trying to convey."

'Yes, sir', we all said unanimously.

'Any doubt' he shouted to us.

'No, sir' we all said together to make an attention posture.

He paused for a second and said, "I'm coming from the office; wait until I do not come, then we'll perform an interesting and brave activity."

'Yes, sir,' we all said simultaneously once again.

The evening was converting into the night rapidly and training had been finished. The other cadets of the unit were leaving the battalion gradually. On the other hand, we were waiting for the *Billa,* outside the battalion office in the N-threes formation. After being silent for over thirty minutes, *Major Tandon* responded, "I think we should move home; he will not come back."

'No' *Major Romeo* answered with dread. "We will wait here and follow the order."

'Yes, sir' both said simultaneously and laughed.

Story 14

The Dream Vendor

The last page of the memories of NCC days

A scene of a tense battlefield where soldiers were advancing, guns were blazing, and explosions were shaking the ground. The air was filled with fear as cries of pain and anguish echoed through the battlefield. The massive noise of artillery and guns was everywhere, drowning out any other sounds. The deafening sounds of explosions and gunfire make it impossible to think straight. The soldiers covered in dirt and sweat and fought desperately for their lives. Their faces were etched with determination and desperation.

The rain was pouring heavily, and we all three were there with our friends inside a trench in INA (Indian National Army) uniform at the forward post of Imphal. Heavy rain turned the battlefield into a muddy quagmire; we were all defending our position with guns in hand. The sound of gunfire echoes through the air, mixing with the pounding rain and creating a chaotic symphony of war. Despite the challenging conditions, our spirits remain unyielding as we stand united, fighting for our country's freedom.

Amid this bustle, *Major Tandon* screamed towards *Major Romeo*, "There is no way out of this hell. We are all going to die here."

"Don't talk like a looser, we are not here to retreat; we will fight until the end" *Major Romeo* replied.

Major Yogi: But it's too late; we can't defeat this foe; it is the mighty British Empire.

"Keep in mind your training," *Major Romeo* shouted. "On the battlefield, the mighty is only the courage."

Major Tandon: But, sir, we don't have any ammunition; our supply line has been cut, and we're dying of hunger.

Major Romeo replied cheerfully, remember what Netaji said: "We will face thirst, hunger, and problems. We will live or die, no problem, but the important thing is that we will ultimately complete our mission, and India will be free."

The whole battalion started shouting, "*Bharat Mata ki Jai, Bharat Mata ki Jai.*"

Suddenly, *Major Tandon* woke up from his peaceful slumber during the class. *Major Tandon* looked around groggily and finally realized he was dreaming. He sighed, relieved, and continued to listen intently to the ongoing lecture. When the lecture ended, *Major Tandon* approached us and shared the vivid details of his dream, igniting a discussion about the sacrifices made by freedom fighters, especially *Subhash Chandra Bose* and the INA. He expressed his admiration for Bose's leadership and the bravery of the soldiers in the Indian National Army.

Major Tandon told *Major Yogi*, "I saw in my dream that we were fighting to Britishers in Imphal, the farthest corner of the country."

Major Yogi: I advise you, please don't watch movies all the time; instead, you should concentrate on your studies and the C certificate exam.

"No, it's not because of too many films," *Major Tandon* replied with a smile. "We both heard the Netaji speech on the radio last week. We haven't been to the movies or the theatre since last month," *Major Tandon* added, pointing to *Major Romeo*.

"Everything is a dream," *Major Romeo* replied, "and what we're doing here, we are living our dream."

"I understand your passion for movies, but it's important to prioritize your goals and responsibilities, and now the NCC C Certificate Exam is my only priority," *Major Yogi* answered gently.

Major Romeo responded, "We are aware; that is why we are here to participate in the three-day training program that *Captain AB* has organized."

Major Yogi: Please take the C certificate exam seriously; it demands training and dedication.

Major Tandon: Yes, *Captain AB* is known for his expertise in the subject; he will clear up all the confusion, so don't worry, we are all in good hands."

Major Yogi added confidently. "I believe this training will greatly enhance our chances of passing the exam with flying colours."

Major Tandon: I have no confusion; I understand the exam structure and grading scale quite well, but I'm frightened to interview.

Major Yogi: Yeah, the interview marks are too high, and we have no idea what they will ask.

Major Romeo: Yes, we need to be well-prepared and confident during the interview. I think we should practice answering potential interview questions and work on our communication skills to make a strong impression.

Major Tandon: "Don't worry, we have solved the written exam course content, and we're doing excellent in drill and parade, so why are we worried?"

"But you are ignoring the importance of shooting." *Santri* abruptly interrupted *Major Romeo*.

"Be careful of your shooting because you got zero marks twice on the firing range," *Major Yogi* answered *Santri*.

Major Tandon unexpectedly advised *Santri*, saying, "You can keep practicing with the toy rifle in your house. It will improve your aiming ability and build confidence on the firing range."

A lot of giggles occurred among the group as they imagined *Santri* practicing with his toy rifle in his room. The environment changed from silliness to order as *Captain AB* showed up out of nowhere. We all arranged ourselves in a disciplined formation and were ready to receive instructions from *Captain AB*.

Captain AB started "Dear cadets, next week you will go for the examination; it will be a 5-day camp where you will give a demonstration of your skill and whatever you have learned in these three years, but remember, the assessment will not only about your skills and strengths; they will also examine your thoughts and attitude. You will appear for examinations like an officer, so always act and think like an officer. Your behaviour and attitude should reflect the expertise and integrity expected of an officer."

In front of the N-threes arrangement on the parade ground, he further inquired, pointing to all three, "What were the interview questions in the B certificate examination?"

Major Romeo said, "What is an ambush, sir?"

Major Yogi said, after remembering something "Which configuration is appropriate for a section when crossing the forest?"

Major Tandon: "What is camouflage?"

Captain AB: And what were your responses?

"An ambush is a surprise attack, sir," *Major Romeo* stated.

Major Yogi explained: The diamond formation is appropriate for search operations.

Major Tandon answered in detail: "Camouflage is the act of hiding or disguising something by covering it up or changing the way it looks."

Captain AB further stated, "The questions, however, will not be as straightforward at this time. They want to know your opinions about the issues. They will evaluate your leadership skills. Consequently, transform yourself from an obedient soldier into an astute officer."

The training had started in the middle of the parade ground, and the cadets were practicing and improving their parade skills. We had all cleared the mock test with flying colours and performed admirably in the drill parade and physical fitness tests. We had started preparing ourselves for the mock interview. In the interview, our ability to think critically and demonstrate leadership qualities will be tested. We memorized answers to some general questions like, 'What is a leader?' and 'What are the characteristics of a leader? How have you nurtured your leadership skills, etc.? could come into the interview.

According to the schedule, we approached the college the next day on time and finished our regular classes. Our interview had finished by the evening, and we all responded differently because we all had our unique perspectives on leadership. Some of us emphasized the importance of communication and the ability to inspire others, while others highlighted qualities such as integrity and adaptability. Overall, we were eager to showcase our abilities and prove that we had what it takes to excel in this role.

After the interview, *Romeo* hurriedly asked *Major Tandon*, "What did you answer about a leader inside the room in front of the interview panel?"

Major Tandon replied, "A leader is a person who is a manager or in charge of something."

Major Romeo asked one more question hastily, "Qualities?"

Major Tandon responds quickly: "Integrity, courage, respect, empathy, and gratitude, as I have memorized from the book."

"What was your response to the leader?" *Major Tandon* asked *Major Romeo* afterward.

Major Romeo reacted hesitantly and masked his response, saying, "No, it's not that important."

The interview concluded with breakfast *Samosas and Rasgullas* as usual, but *Captain AB's* remarks highlighted the overall potential of the cadets, acknowledging their competence but also emphasizing the need for improvement. He concluded that most of the cadets are efficient and will pass the examination, but most of them need improvement. He pointed his finger toward the *Santri* and said, "There is no relationship between dinner and leadership; leadership relates to responsibility, not to dinner. Please correct yourself." This incident stopped *Santri* amid his *samosa*, which made all the cadets laugh. Finally, he extended his best wishes and encouragement to the cadets, expressing his confidence in their ability to conquer their weaknesses and succeed in their future endeavours.

In the end, all the qualified applicants participated in the examination that was eagerly anticipated, but only four cadets passed the C certificate exam. We were all happy because we had the certificate in our hands, but others may have hope because the army also gave them a second chance. However, the Indian Army employed a testing format in which candidates who failed got a second attempt with a higher level of difficulty. This format allows cadets to demonstrate their resilience and ability to overcome challenges. It also ensures that those who ultimately pass the exam have truly earned their certification and are well-prepared for future responsibilities.

The result of our hard work and dedication was evident when we received our scores, which exceeded our expectations and filled us with a sense of pride and accomplishment. The high scores not only validated our efforts but also boosted our confidence in our abilities. Despite the disappointment, the other cadets remained motivated and determined to continue their efforts toward success in their future endeavours.

Our battalion was giving us a fantastic farewell party for our batch to celebrate our achievements and acknowledge our dedication. It was a heartwarming party that further solidified our bond as we prepared to embark on different paths in our lives. We were having a great time dancing and laughing together, reminiscing about the challenges we had overcome and the memories we had created. The camaraderie and support within our battalion were evident as we cheered each other on and celebrated our collective success. We were overjoyed because we had the certificate, but others were optimistic.

That day, we donned our uniforms and ranks for the last time, symbolizing the end of our shared journey and the beginning of our paths. As we stood together, proud, and united, we couldn't help but feel a sense of bittersweetness, knowing that our time as a tight-knit unit was coming to an end. However, we were filled with excitement and anticipation for the new challenges and opportunities that awaited us on our future paths.

In his farewell message, *Captain AB* stated, "Boys, Remember, this certificate is not merely a symbol of discipline and patriotism; you are an NCC soldier for life. The values and skills you learned in the NCC will stay with you no matter what path you take in the future. You will join the army or civil service, but I hope you will carry the spirit of the NCC with you in all aspects of your life. I am confident that each of you will make a positive impact in your workplace. In the future, you may become an army officer, police officer, or teacher, but regardless of the path you choose, the discipline and patriotism instilled in you through your NCC training will undoubtedly contribute to your success. The values of teamwork, leadership, and dedication that you have cultivated will serve as a strong foundation for any profession you pursue. Our country is indeed facing many problems; our enemy is not only on the border but also within our society. In this crucial situation, you will become my small but powerful army, which will fight not only on the borders but also on critical fronts within society. Good luck, and may we meet again on the path of service to our nation."

Amid *Captain AB's* farewell message, *Major Tandon* started dreaming again, and this time he saw his brave army troop fighting with enemies on a mountain ridge. *Major Tandon*'s army was well-equipped and eager to fight, and his soldiers were advancing, guns blazing, and explosions shaking the ground. The massive noise of artillery and guns was everywhere, drowning out any other sounds. Abruptly, *Major Tandon* advanced toward the enemy with his SLR, leading his troops with unwavering determination. The intense battle raged on, and *Major Tandon* opened fire on the opponents with his beloved SLR. His shots were precise and deadly, taking down enemy soldiers one by one. He was just about to win, but as he turned around to celebrate his victory, an enemy bullet hit *Major Romeo*, and he rolled down the hill. *Major Tandon*'s heart sank as he witnessed *Major Romeo*'s fall, but suddenly another bullet hit *Major Yogi*, one of *Major Tandon*'s closest friends. They were both no longer visible on the battlefield and in the same manner, the other cadets and friends also vanished.

The dream has ended, and we have all returned to our normal lives, but the dream vendor remains at the same location.

Important Information

- **Battalion:** A battalion is a military unit that consists of 300 to 1,000 soldiers.
- **Section:** A section is a primary unit of the military. It usually consists of 10 soldiers.
- **Platoon:** A platoon is a military unit comprising two to four sections or patrols.
- **Artillery:** Artillery in the army refers to the combat arm that provides firepower during ground operations. Artillery can also refer to the soldiers who operate the weapons.
- **Tank division:** A tank division is a military formation that is made up of tanks and other armored vehicles.
- **Infantry:** Members of the infantry are ground troops that engage with the enemy in close-range combat.
- **Codes in Army:** Alpha, Bravo, Charlie, Delta, Echo, Foxtrot, Golf, Hotel, India, Juliett, Kilo, Lima, Mike, November, Oscar, Papa, Quebec,

Romeo, Sierra, Tango, Uniform, Victor, Whiskey, X-ray, Yankee, Zulu.

- **Snake Trench:** A snake trench should be marked with a line, one foot wide, and three feet from the tent's outer edge on all sides.

Ranks in Senior Division NCC

All others who joined NCC are commonly called as Cadets.

Ranks in the Army

Non-commissioned officer

Sepoy

Lance Naik

Naik

Havildar

Junior commissioned officer

Naib Subedar

Subedar

Subedar Major

Commissioned officer

Lieutenant

Captain

Major

Lieutenant Colonel

Colonel

Brigadier

Major General

Lieutenant General

General

Field Marshel

NCC Song

Hum Sab Bharatiya Hain, Hum Sab Bharatiya Hain

Apni Manzil Ek Hai,

Ha, Ha, Ha, Ek Hai,

Ho, Ho, Ho, Ek Hai.

Hum Sab Bharatiya Hain.

Kashmir Ki Dharti Rani Hai,

Sartaj Himalaya Hai,

Saadiyon Se Humne Isko Apne Khoon Se Pala Hai

Desh Ki Raksha Ki Khatir Hum Shamshir Utha Lenge,

Hum Shamshir Utha Lenge.

Bikhre Bikhre Taare Hain Hum Lekin Jhilmil Ek Hai,

Ha, Ha, Ha, Ek Hai

Hum Sab Bharatiya Hai.

Mandir Gurudwaare Bhi Hain Yahan

Aur Masjid Bhi Hai Yahan

Girija Ka Hai Ghariyaal Kahin

Mullah ki Kahin Hai Ajaan

Ek Hi Apna Ram Hain, Ek hi Allah Taala Hai,

Ek Hi Allah Taala Hain, Rang Birange Deepak Hain Hum,

lekin Jagmag Ek Hai, Ha Ha Ha Ek Hai, Ho Ho Ho Ek Hai.

Hum Sab Bharatiya Hain, Hum Sab Bharatiya Hain.

THE NCC UNIFORM

The Uniform is an integral part of the National Cadet Corps.
It represents a sense of dignity, responsibility and immense pride
of being a cadet and a caterer to the responsibilities of a good citizen.

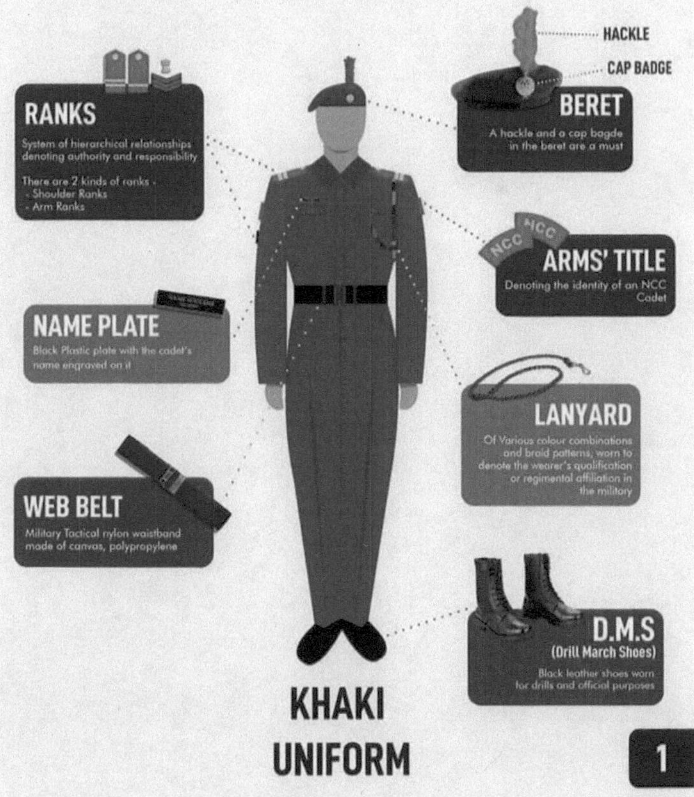

www.ingramcontent.com/pod-product-compliance
Lightning Source LLC
LaVergne TN
LVHW041214150826
845673LV00001B/400

* 9 7 9 8 8 9 2 7 7 8 7 0 1 *